Anonymous

Niagara

SALZWASSER
VERLAG

Anonymous

Niagara

Reprint of the original, first published in 1859.

1st Edition 2022 | ISBN: 978-3-37513-188-3

Verlag (Publisher): Salzwasser Verlag GmbH, Zeilweg 44, 60439 Frankfurt, Deutschland
Vertretungsberechtigt (Authorized to represent): E. Roepke, Zeilweg 44, 60439 Frankfurt, Deutschland
Druck (Print): Books on Demand GmbH, In de Tarpen 42, 22848 Norderstedt, Deutschland

SUSPENSION BRIDGE, FALLS OF NIAGARA.

NIAGARA SUSPENSION BRIDGE—RAILROAD TRACK VIEW.

THE FALLS OF NIAGARA.

[Distant from New York, 440; Quebec, 585; Philadelphia, 441; Baltimore, 632; Toronto, 50; Buffalo, 22 miles.]

To attempt to convey the faintest impression of the unspeakable magnitude and magnificence of the Falls of Niagara almost borders on presumption. They have been clad with a brilliant halo of imagination since we first heard of their existence, at school. The pen, the pencil, and photography, have all been laid under contribution, for the purpose of describing and illustrating the mighty cataract. The powers of word-painting have been wielded by the literateur, the preacher, and the poet, to furnish suitable representations of the "world's wonder." Futility and failure have been written upon every attempt. The thunder of waters is inexpressible by human language; but yet, to be admired it needs only to be seen; and the deep impression that is stamped upon the mind of every spectator that stands before the stupendous scene of Niagara, will never be erased from the tablets of memory. Who shall ever forget that moment when he leapt from the cars, bounded, with all the impatience of a curiosity cherished from earliest infancy, down the declivity, and the sublime scene burst upon his astonished vision?

The eye wandered up and down "the Rapids," rushing, for a mile above the Falls, in tumultuous madness, fretting and eddying, whirling and twirling, rumbling and tumbling, pell-mell, in precipitate confusion; fell then upon the pure, pellucid waters, that soothed themselves into a solemn sweep as they moved, with the majesty of irresistible might over the lofty precipice, with the deafening roar of gratulation at their safe descent; and last, not least, upon the beauteous bow that capped and crowned the glowing scene resplendent with magnificence and redolent of transcendent sublimity.

But instead of straining the capabilities of language, by heaping metaphor on metaphor, in a listless endeavour to describe the indescribable, let us act as *cicerone* to the tourist, and leave him to drink inspiration from the voice of the living waters themselves.

We may here notice that the Falls are formed by the United waters of Lake Superior, Lake Michigan, Lake Huron, and Lake Erie, which all meet in the River Niagara, at the eastern extremity of Lake Erie, from which it pursues its

8

stream, than for any great similarity to an immense whirlpool, which many expect to see.

The best view, however, of the Whirlpool is to be had at the edge of the river, on the American side, exactly opposite to the point mentioned above. To reach there, you proceed across the Suspension Bridge, turn to your left, and walk along the public road till you reach Devaux's College—which you cannot but observe as you go along. There you turn from off the public road, and follow a narrow road through a dense wood, until you reach a small wooden house, where you will find parties ready to give you all information respecting the path down to the edge of the river below. You there pay 25 cents, which goes to the support of Devaux's College—a college established, at a cost of $154,000, by a Frenchman named Devaux, for the free maintenance and education of 100 boys. You will, in all probability, be pleased with your visit to the Whirlpool. Whilst there, you may proceed to the Devil's Hole, a short way down the river, on the same side, and which consists of a chasm of about 200 feet deep on the bank of the river. The small stream which pours over the precipice above there, is called Bloody Run—named so in consequence of the colour given to it on one occasion by the blood of the British troops mixing with it, during an engagement with some Indians and French during the war there in 1763.

BROCK'S MONUMENT forms one of the "lions" of Niagara, which tourists, in approaching from Toronto, per steamer and rail, will observe to great advantage, as they proceed in the cars from the town of Niagara to Suspension Bridge. It stands on Queenstown Heights (Canada side). Erected to the British general, Sir Isaac Brock, who fell in the engagement fought there in 1812. On the top stands the statue of the gallant officer. Although a considerable distance from the Falls, (about 7 miles,) yet if the tourist has time, the visit to it will repay the time and trouble, as a most magnificent view of the river, country round about, and Lake Ontario is there obtained.

Opposite Queenstown, on the River Niagara, is Lewiston—famous for its stupendous suspension bridge—even longer than the one further up the river, being 1045 feet long.

NIAGARA FALLS.—In addition to the name of the celebrated Falls, the town in the immediate vicinity takes also the name of Niagara Falls—situated in the State of New York.

As is well known, it is the fashionable resort of all who desire to make their residence on the American side of the river. The hotels are on the largest scale, and characterized by great magnificence and comfort. Trains arrive at and depart from the station at the town, to and from which omnibuses run in connection with the principal hotels.

The town on the American side, at Suspension Bridge, is known by the name of Niagara City.

Travellers for the Falls should check their baggage to "Niagara Falls," if they intend residing on the American side; and to "Suspension Bridge, Clifton," if on the Canadian side—on which side there are excellent hotels also.

The large illustration of the Falls given in a previous page, was taken from what is considered the best point for seeing both the American and Canadian (or Horse-Shoe) Falls together, viz., near the Clifton House, on the Canadian side of the river. This view was taken by photograph, by M. Hufnagel, photographer, Broadway, New York, last summer, and is decidedly the best and most correct view of the Falls we ever saw on paper. To preserve as far as possible, in the process of engraving, all the details of the great original, we have had M. Hufnagel's immense photograph re-photographed on a reduced scale on wood, by Price's patent process, and engraved, so that we can, with confidence, refer to the accompanying view of the Niagara Falls as correct in every particular.

The other illustrations, excepting the "bird's-eye view," have also been engraved from photographs.

ROUTES TO THE FALLS.

There are several routes from the Atlantic seaboard, the best of which we give, with the distances and fare, as near as can be ascertained; as also one from Quebec through Canada:—

FROM NEW YORK.

No. 1.

	Miles.	Cost.
Steamer, from New York to Albany	150	$1.50
Rail, from Albany to Rochester	229	4.58
Rail, from Rochester to Niagara Falls	76	1.52
Total	455	$7.60

£1 10s. 6d. stg.

From New York to Albany the Hudson River Railroad can be taken; distance, 144 miles; fare, $3.00.

No. 2.

	Miles.	Cost.
N. York and Erie R. R. to Hornellsville	338	$6.75
Rail, from Hornellsville to Buffalo	91	2.10
Rail, from Buffalo to Niagara Falls	22	0.60
Total	446	$9.45

£1 18s. stg.

Or, per New York and Erie Railroad to Rochester and Buffalo direct, 298 miles, thence as above.

FROM NEW YORK.

No. 3.

	Miles.	Cost.
New York and Erie Railroad to Elmira	274	$6.00
Rail, from Elmira to Niagara Falls	166	4.10
Total	440	$10.10

£2 0s. 6d. stg.

FROM QUEBEC.

No. 4.

	Miles.	Cost.
Rail, to Montreal	171	$6.00
Rail, from Montreal to Toronto	333	10.00
Rail, from Toronto to Niagara Falls	81	1.83
Total	585	$17.83

£3 11s. 6d. stg.

From Toronto the steamer can be taken to Niagara, (36 miles,) on Lake Ontario; thence rail (14 miles) to Suspension Bridge. Total distance, from Toronto, about 50 miles; cost, $1.50 (6s. stg.).

VIEW OF GENESEE FALLS, NEAR PORTAGE,

STATE OF NEW YORK.

THE name of Genesee is one of the household words of Great Britain as well as America. From the Genesee district thousands of barrels of flour, made from its world-renowned wheat, finds its way to England every year, the best proof of the well-known richness of the soil of the Genesee Valley, of which the above engraving represents one of its most striking features.

The Railroad Bridge, seen in the background, is a magnificent structure, for the purpose of enabling the Buffalo & New York City Railroad to cross the valley. Situated about a mile from the village of Genesee Falls, this bridge spans the valley by its entire length of 800 feet, with a height, from the bed of the river, of 234 feet. The precipices in the vicinity are, in some places, 400 feet high.

Genesee Falls consist of a series of falls situated at different points. Near Rochester, they are about 100 feet high. Whilst another fall is about the same height over the mouth of the river. The point we have selected for engraving from a photograph, represents one of the series of falls—from one of the most picturesque spots in the Genesee Valley— viz., above the saw mill, near Portage.

Genesee Falls are much visited by tourists every year.

Rochester is one of the leading stations, leading from New York to Suspension Bridge and Niagara Falls, so that tourists can easily visit the Falls of the Genesee on their way to the Falls, par excellence.

Toronto, the second most important city in Canada. This city presents a much finer appearance from the lake than when approached by railway. Toronto boasts of a large number of fine buildings and elegant churches, as well as of extensive and tasteful blocks of business stores; and the beauty of their appearance is much enhanced by the large number of trees, and the quantity of shrubbery that adorns many of its streets. King street, its principal thoroughfare, is two miles long, and is lined on both sides with handsome stores and public buildings.

Leaving Toronto, the first town of any particular note, on the Canadian side, is Port Whitby, 29 miles below. This is the chief town in Ontario County, and contains near 4,000 inhabitants. It is a station on the Grand Trunk Railway, and is a stopping-place for steamers from Toronto to Rochester, etc.

Oshawa, 4 miles below, is a fine town of 3,000 inhabitants, on the Grand Trunk Railroad, and communicating with the interior towns by lines of stages. A great quantity of flour is shipped from here.

Bowmanville, 10 miles below, lies a little back of the lake, to which it is connected by *Darlington Harbour*. In 1850, the place was incorporated a village, since which period its growth has been very rapid. The town has excellent water power within and around it. The country around is unsurpassed for fertility and salubrity by any in Canada. It has a population of about 5,000.

Port Hope is about 20 miles below Bowmanville, and, like it, is a station on the Grand Trunk Railroad. It is also connected by railway with Lindsay, 40 miles, and with Peterborough, 29 miles distant. Steamers also ply between this place and several towns lying north, on Lake Sturgeon. Port Hope is built on an acclivity, the summit of which is capped with beach and pine, and clothed with villas, embowered among the trees. The principal street runs from the harbour to the top of the hill, and is lined with elegant stores, beautiful dwellings and commodious hotels. The Town Hall and Montreal Bank form prominent objects to a spectator placed upon the quay. And the graceful

above, old Fort Niagara, at the mouth of the river, and which possesses a fine natural harbour, open at all seasons of the year. The river is here about half a mile in width, across which a ferry plies to the village of Niagara, on the Canadian side.

Fort Niagara.—In passing into the lake, this old relic of former times is especially noticeable. As early as 1679, this spot was inclosed by La Salle, the explorer of the Mississippi. In 1725, a pallisade fort was constructed by the French. In 1759, it was taken by the British, who, in 1796, gave it into the hands of the Americans. In 1813, it was taken again by the British, and recaptured by the Americans in 1815. There is no doubt that the dungeons of this old fort have been the scenes of horrible suffering and of crime, from the times of the old Indian and French wars, up to the days of the Revolution. In its close and impregnable dungeons, the light of day never shone; and here, doubtless, many a poor prisoner has been compelled to undergo the "torture," in addition to his other nameless sufferings.

As, after entering the lake, no place of much importance is reached for some hours, the tourist should embrace this opportunity of getting a good view of the scenes he is about leaving. On a clear day, a fine view is presented of Brock's Monument, and the grand heights of Queenstown, 9 or 10 miles distant, which rise nearly 500 feet above the waters of the lake.

After passing several small settlements, we reach

Charlotte, or Port Genesee, at the mouth of the River Genesee, port of entry for Rochester, 7 miles distant, and 87 miles from Niagara. This town possesses a safe harbour, being protected by two long piers, on one of which is located a lighthouse. A number of steamers run daily from here to several of the principal places on both sides of the lake.

The Falls of Genesee.—These beautiful falls, second only to Niagara, are objects worthy of notice. The banks of the Genesee, just above Charlotte, rise from 50 to 150 feet in height. The river is navigable as far as Carthage, which may be called a suburb of Rochester. From this lake, as it is the first important island met, in the passage from the head of the lake, on the Canada side. In former years, immense quantities of wild ducks gathered upon this island, and hence its name.

AMHERST ISLAND, also belonging to Canada, lies a little further on. It is a large body of very fertile land, which is under a good state of cultivation. Beyond this island, we come to the end of the lake, and soon enter the mouth of the St. Lawrence River. We now pass two islands—*Gage* and *Wolf*—which are the first of that astonishing group known as the "Thousand Islands." We next come to KINGSTON, which is probably the finest-looking city in Canada, although not doing a business equal to Montreal or Toronto. A tourist, speaking of this city, says:

"The view of the city and surrounding scenery is not surpassed by the approaches to any other city in America. A few miles above Kingston, the waters of Lake Ontario are divided by the first of the long series of islands so well known to tourists as the 'Thousand Islands,' of which Simcoe and Grand, or Wolfe Islands, opposite the city, may be looked upon as strongholds designed by nature to withstand the encroaches of the waves of Ontario. On approaching from the west, by water, the first object that attracts the traveller's attention is *Fort Henry*, with the naval station of *Fort Frederick* at its base, and its attendant battlements, fortifications, towers and redoubts."

FORT HENRY is a favourite resort for visitors, and its elevated position affords the best view that can be had of the city, lake and surrounding country.

The principal public buildings are the City Hall, Court-House, Roman Catholic Cathedral, Queen's College, Roman Catholic College, General Hospital, Penitentiary, 16 or 18 fine churches, banking-houses, etc. The City Hall is one of the finest edifices in Canada, built of cut lime-stone, at an expense of near $100,000. It has a spacious hall, holding over 1,000 persons. There are 20 steamers, and about 50 sailing vessels, owned here; and these, besides other Canadian and American craft, are mostly occupied in

River, at its entrance into Lake Ontario, and is the largest and most active city on the lake. There are from 15 to 20 flour-ing-mills, making over 10,000 barrels of flour per day, when in operation, and about a dozen elevators, with storage-room for 2,000,000 bushels of grain. It is handsomely built, with streets 100 feet wide, crossing each other at right angles. The river divides the city into nearly two equal parts, which are connected by two bridges, above ship navigation.

The number of vessels which arrive and depart from this port is very large. It is estimated that one-half of the entire trade of Canada with the United States is carried on with Oswego. A railroad, 36 miles in length, connects Oswego with Syracuse. The Oswego Canal also connects at Syracuse with the Erie Canal. Oswego ranks as one of the greatest grain markets in the world, being second on this continent only to Chicago. From her position, she must continue to hold her advantage, and, in spite of all rivalry, will always command the greatest portion of Canadian trade. The population of Oswego is about 20,000.

Leaving Oswego, we pass *Mexico Bay*, into which empties

SALMON RIVER, at the mouth of which is a small town, called *Port Ontario*. *Salmon River Falls* are classed among the greatest natural curiosities of the country. The current of the river is disturbed, about 6 miles from its mouth, by 2 miles of rapids, which terminate in a fall of 107 feet. At high water, the sheet is 250 feet in width, but, at low water, is narrowed to about half that extent. At the foot of the falls the water is very deep, and abounds in fine fish, such as salmon, trout and bass.

SACKETT'S HARBOUR, 45 miles north of Oswego, possesses one of the most secure harbours on the lake. During the war of 1812, with England, it was used as the rendezvous of the American fleet on Lake Ontario. A large war-vessel, commenced at that time, still remains here under cover. Madison Barracks, garrisoned by United States troops, is situated near the landing.

BLACK RIVER, just beyond, is 120 miles long, but its navigation is much impeded by a succession of rapids and falls. It

CHANNEL OF THE ST. LAWRENCE.

STEAMER DESCENDING ONE OF THE RAPIDS OF THE ST. LAWRENCE.

each year a body of trained *voyageurs* set out hence in large canoes, called *maitres canots*, with packages and goods for the various posts in the wilderness. Two centuries ago, the companions of the explorer Cartier, on arriving here, thought they had discovered a route to China, and expressed their joy in the exclamation of La Chine! Hence the present name, or so at least says tradition."

to be met with on the steamers, and in the streets in the cities of Montreal, Quebec, and even in New York, selling their fancy bead-work, etc.

La Prairie is some seven miles below Caughnawaga, or Village of the Rapids, after which the steamer sails on for a few miles, and reaches the City of Montreal.

LACHINE RAPIDS.

PREVIOUS to entering the Lachine Rapids, the tourist may observe the entrance to the aqueduct of the water-works which supplies Montreal with water—a gigantic undertaking, and affording the citizens of that city a never-failing, unlimited supply of good *aqua*.

There are 7 small islands in the channel of the Lachine Rapids. The steamer passes on between Isle du Diable, Isle au Heron, and Isle Boket, and after passing down the rapids, the steamer proceeds along, passing near to Nun's Island, belonging to the Grey Nunnery, Montreal, and one of the many islands which belong, and yield large resources to, the nunneries. A slight rapid, named

NORMAN RAPID, is sailed through, and, after passing that great monument of engineering skill, the Victoria Bridge, the steamer lands her passengers at the wharf of the city of Montreal.

84

Proceeding on for other eight miles, the steamer stops at one of the oldest settled towns in Canada, viz.:

THREE RIVERS, 90 miles from Montreal, being half way between Quebec and Montreal. Situated at the confluence of the St. Lawrence and River St. Maurice. Population about 5000. The most prominent buildings are the Roman Catholic and Protestant churches, a convent, jail, and court-house. Founded in 1618. After leaving Three Rivers the steamer proceeds onwards, and shortly passes the mouth of the St. Maurice River, which enters the St. Lawrence from Canada. The beautiful stream runs a course of some 400 miles in a south-east direction, frequently expanding and forming lakes of various sizes. Its banks are generally very high, varying from 200 to 1,000 feet, and covered with thick groups of variegated trees. It has a number of falls and cascades, and is adorned with several small islands. Its principal tributaries are the Ribbon and Vermillion, running from the west, and the Windigo and Croche Rivers, from the east. The next town reached is

BATISCAN, on the same side of the river, 117 miles from Montreal, and the last stopping-place before arriving at Quebec. Batiscan is reached at an early hour in the morning.

RICHELIEU RAPIDS.—The channel of the river where these rapids occur is very narrow and intricate, huge irregular rocks being visible in many places during low water. Beacon lights are placed at the most dangerous points, to aid the mariner in navigating these difficult passages, which extend a distance of 8 or 9 miles.

Pursuing our course, we pass the small settlements of St. Marie, St. Anne, Point Aux Trembles, and Port Neuf, on t. · north, and Gentilly, St. Pierre, Dechellons, Lothinière, and St. Croix, on the south side of the river. Nearly opposite St. Croix is Cape Sante.

CAPE SANTE is about 30 miles above Quebec, on the north side of the river; a small settlement called St. Trois being on the opposite shore. The banks of the river rise here almost perpendicularly to a height of 80 feet above the water, and extend back for many miles with an almost level surface.

CAPE ROUGE, 8 miles above Quebec, is next passed on the left, when the citadel of Quebec comes into view, presenting a sight at once grand and deeply interesting, from its historical associations.

CHAUDIERE RIVER, on the right, has a number of beautiful falls a short distance from its entrance into the St. Lawrence.

WOLF'S COVE, 2 miles above Quebec, is historically famous as the place where the immortal *Wolfe* landed with his gallant army in 1759, and ascended to the Plains of Abraham, where the heroic chief fell mortally wounded, just at the successful termination of one of the most daring enterprises ever chronicled in the annals of warfare.

On the opposite side of the river is Point Levi, a small town of about 1500 inhabitants. Here is the Quebec station of the Grand Trunk Railroad.

On approaching Quebec the character of the country again resumes a more picturesque appearance—the high banks and finely-wooded country showing to great advantage. Within a few miles of the City of Quebec some private residences may be seen embosomed amid the foliage, in romantic situations, on the heights above, on the north side of the river, and on nearing the city the port of New Liverpool may be seen on the right-hand, or south side of the river, with some large ships lying at anchor there, as well as all the way between there and Quebec; where, during the season of open navigation, immense numbers of large vessels may be seen waiting to discharge their cargoes, and load the timber of Canada for transportation to all parts of the world, but more particularly to Greenock, on the River Clyde, (Scotland,) and Liverpool, on the Mersey, (England).

Previous to arriving, the spot may be seen on the face of the embankment where the gallant Montgomery was killed whilst attempting to storm the citadel at that point.

The steamer, after rounding the high cliffs and Cape Diamond, takes a sweep round in the river, and lands its passengers, about seven o'clock in the morning, at the base of the Citadel of Quebec—the "Gibraltar of America."

OTTAWA, CANADA WEST.—LOWER, AND PART OF CENTRAL, TOWN.

NIAGARA;

ITS

FALLS AND SCENERY:

TOGETHER WITH

𝕿𝖍𝖊 𝖂𝖍𝖎𝖙𝖊 𝕸𝖔𝖚𝖓𝖙𝖆𝖎𝖓𝖘,

GENESEE FALLS, TRENTON FALLS, MONTMORENCI FALLS,
RIVER OTTAWA, RIVER SAGUENAY,

THE CITY OF QUEBEC,

AND

RÓUTE DOWN THE ST. LAWRENCE.

THE WHOLE DESCRIBED AND

ILLUSTRATED WITH THIRTY-FOUR ENGRAVINGS.

———•••———

NEW YORK:
ALEX. HARTHILL, 20 NORTH WILLIAM STREET;
ROSS & TOUSEY; H. DEXTER & CO.; HENDRICKSON, BLAKE & LONG.
TORONTO:—McLEAR & CO. MONTREAL:—D. DAWSON & SON.
And Sold by all Booksellers and Newsmen.

CONTENTS.

LIST OF ILLUSTRATIONS.

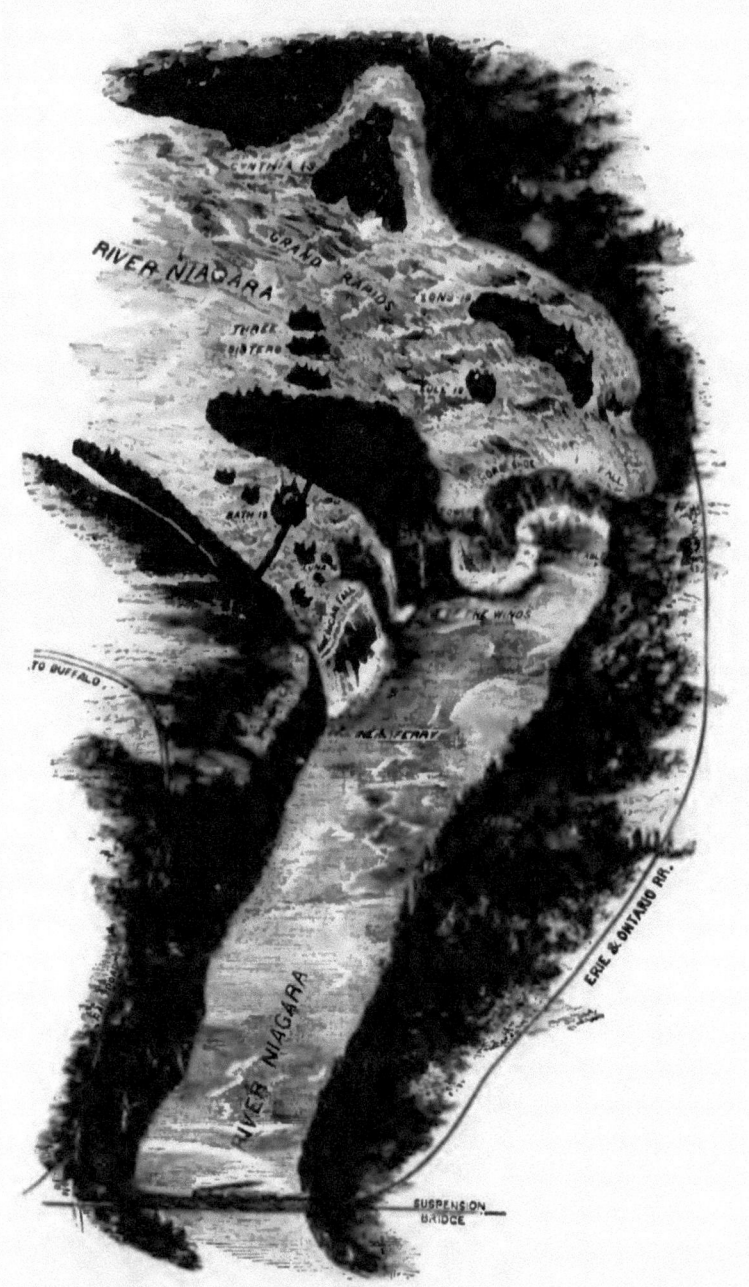

BIRD'S-EYE VIEW OF NIAGARA.

THE NIAGARA SUSPENSION BRIDGE.

NIAGARA SUSPENSION BRIDGE.

The above sketch represents the great International Bridge, which spans the Niagara, and joins the United States with Canada. Its length, from tower to tower, is 821 feet 4 inches. Erected at a cost of about $400,000 (£80,000 stg.). The lower floor or road-way is used for foot passengers, carriages, carts, etc., same as any ordinary road. The upper floor is for railroad traffic exclusively. Across this bridge, the trains of the Great Western Railroad of Canada and the various railroads of New York State, travel, each train drawn very slowly, by a light pilot engine.

From a report, by Mr. Roebling, Engineer, on this gigantic structure, we copy the following particulars:—

"The base and towers on the New York side, contain 1350 cubic yards, which weigh about 3,000 tons. Add to this weight of the superstructure of 1,000 tons, and we have a total of 4,000 tons, in a compact and solid mass.

"There are 4 cables of 10 inches diameter, each composed of 3640 wires of small No. 9

6

gauge, 60 wires forming one square inch of solid section; making the solid section of each cable 60.40 square inches, wrapping not included.

"Each of the four large cables is composed of seven smaller ones, which I call *strands*. Each strand contains 520 wires. One of these forms the centre, the six others are placed around it—the 520 wires forming one strand of endless wire, obtained by splicing a number of single wires. The ends of the strands are passed around and confined in cast-iron shoes, which also receive the wrought-iron pin that forms a connection with the anchor chains.

"The wire measures 18.31 feet per pound, and the strength, therefore, is equivalent to 1640 lbs. per single wire, or nearly 100,000 pounds per square inch.

"Assuming the above average strength, the aggregate strength of the 14,560 wires composing the four cables, will be 23,878,400 pounds. But their actual strength is greater, because the above calculations are based upon a *minimum* strength of the individual wires. We may assume their aggregate ultimate strength at 12,000 tons, of 2,000 pounds each.

"Both ends of the bridge rest upon the cliffs, and are anchored to the rock. As far as supported by the cables, I estimate its weight at less than 1000 tons, which includes the weight of cables between the towers, and is a pressure of the river stays below.

"There are 624 suspenders, each capable of sustaining thirty tons, which makes their united strength 18,720 tons. The ordinary weight they have to support is only 1000 tons. A locomotive of thirty-four tons weight, including tender, spreads its weight, by means of the girders and trusses, over a length of no less than 200 feet. Of course the greatest pressure is under the engine, and is there supported by no less than twenty suspenders. If, by any accident, a sudden blow or jar should be produced, the strength of the suspenders will be abundant to meet it.

"A change of temperature of 100° causes a difference in the level of the floor of two feet three inches. The lower floor, or river stays have enough of slack, or deflection, to adjust themselves under these changes. The only difference will be, that they are tighter in winter than in summer; consequently, that the equilibrium of the bridge will be less affected by passing trains in cold weather than in warm.

"Droves of cattle are, according to the regulations, to be divided off into troops of 20, no more than three such bodies, or 60 in all, to be allowed on the bridge at one time. Each troop is to be led by one person, who is to check their progress in case they should start off on a trot.

"In my opinion, a heavy train, running at a speed of 20 miles an hour, does less injury to the structure, than is caused by 20 heavy cattle under a full trot. Public processions, marching to the sound of music, or bodies of soldiers keeping regular step, will produce a still more injurious effect."

The charge for passing over the bridge, on foot, is 25 cents—going and returning. Carriage $1.00, with 25 cents for each passenger inside.

The promenade, during a hot day, on the foot-path of the bridge, is deliciously cool, from the breeze which generally blows up or down the gorge of the river. The views looking towards the Falls, from different points on the bridge, are also exceedingly good, presenting to the stranger the picture of Niagara Falls, as they are represented in many engravings which are given of them, and even the best of them, after all, only can give a very faint idea of the great reality.

Suspension Bridge is the station where all the emigrant trains bound for the western states stay over—generally for some hours. Refreshment rooms to suit all classes are to be met with both inside and outside of the railroad station. Average charge, 25 cents per meal.

7

AMERICAN FALL.

GOAT ISLAND.

HORSE-SHOE FALL.

FALLS OF NIAGARA.

course for about 22 miles, where it is divided, by Goat Island, into two falls—the one forming a fall in a straight line, called the AMERICAN FALL, as it falls on the United States side of the River, and the other in a sort of semi-circular form, or, as it has been called the HORSE-SHOE FALL, on the Canada side of the river.

The American Fall is about 900 feet wide, with a descent, in one unbroken sheet, of 163 feet perpendicular.

The Canadian or Horse-Shoe Fall is about 2000 feet wide, with a fall of 158 feet. The total descent of the water from Lake Erie to Lake Ontario is 334 feet. Such is the great action of the water upon the precipice over which it falls—as well as upon the embankments upon both sides of the river—it is estimated that about one foot is worn away annually, and that the falls have receded during the course of ages—estimated by geologists at 37,000 years—from Queenstown, 7 miles below, to where they are at present.

With these preliminary remarks, we shall proceed to describe the most important objects of interest, addressing ourselves as if the reader were on a visit there

As one very common route for strangers who wish to "do" the Falls in the most methodical and particular manner, we subjoin the following, which can be adopted, either in whole or in part, by the tourist, as he may feel disposed.

Supposing, then, that you are on the American side of the river, you proceed to GOAT ISLAND. In proceeding thither you cross the bridge of 8 arches, which spans the river, to Bath Island, from off which you get an excellent view of the Rapids, as they come rushing along, as if bent on sweeping away the bridge, and every thing on it, before them down the stream and over the fall. Arrived across the bridge, you enter a cottage, register your name, and pay a toll of 25 cents, (1s. stg.,) which will admit you to cross and recross during the whole season. Passing on, you may observe, to your right hand, the paper works which were burned down last autumn. Passing them, you cross another small bridge, and then enter upon the beautiful grounds of Goat Island. Turning to the right hand, you proceed to the "Hog's Back," and across a small bridge to "Luna Island," which divides a small portion of the American Fall. An excellent view is there obtained of the American Fall, and scenery up and down the river.

After leaving Luna Island, you proceed through Goat Island, keeping on the walk nearest the river, towards the Canadian Fall. Before reaching there, however, you descend Biddle's Stairs (named after Mr. Biddle, of Philadelphia, who built them) to the Cave of the Winds.

CAVE OF THE WINDS.—Reaching the bottom of Biddle's Stairs you proceed by a narrow foot path towards the American Fall, behind which the Cave is situated. There you are provided with a waterproof dress, and obtain a magnificent view of the Fall as it thunders down from above and in front of you. Charge for loan of dress, $1.00 (4s. stg.). The Cave is 130 feet high, 100 feet wide, and 30 feet deep.

Retracing your steps to Biddle's Stairs, but before reascending them, you can have an excellent view of the Horse-Shoe Fall, as seen from the edge of the river. After regaining the top of these stairs you may be disposed to rest. Plenty of seats are to be found close at hand, where you may rest and admire the scene around and in front of you. Proceeding from there, you now follow the path towards the grandest point of all, the Terrapin Bridge, (Terrapin signifies Turtle,) and Prospect Tower. (See engraving.)

TERRAPIN BRIDGE, AND PROSPECT TOWER.—Arrived at the edge of the river, as it sweeps rapidly past, you proceed along the wooden bridge, which extends to the base of the Tower. At every step, you may be apt to pause and admire the grandeur of the scene. From the base of the Tower a magnificent view of the river and rapids are to be seen; but you now ascend to the top of Prospect Tower, up through a narrow spiral staircase, and, once outside on the top, it is then and there, in our opinion, that the true grandeur of the Horse-Shoe Fall is to be seen, as its mighty volume of 670,000 tons of water comes rushing along every minute, and falls with a continuous roar over the precipice of 158 feet deep, down into the gorge below, where the river has been estimated to be 250 feet deep. The vast volume of water—the magnificent view down the river to Suspension Bridge—the rapids coming down the cataract behind you—together with the scenery on every side—will all combine to entrance you to the spot with admiration and delight, and render you almost unwilling to leave a scene so grand and inspiring.

Retracing your steps towards Goat Island, you next proceed to the Three Sisters—three islands which stand out in the river, and named, respectively, "Moss Island," "Deer Island," and "Allan's Island." Between the first of the Three Sisters and Goat Island is the "Hermit's Cascade," named after a religious hermit, who became so enamoured with the spot that he took up his abode and lived there for some time, in Robinson Crusoe fashion, till one day he was non est, it being supposed he had ventured too far upon a particular log of wood, which capsized him into a watery grave.

The walk around Goat Island will be highly appreciated. Some charming nooks of great beauty are there, whilst from the head of the Island is to be seen, 2½ miles up the river, Chippewa; and, four miles from there, Navy Island, belonging to Canada, which was occupied by the Canadian patriots of 1837-8. From there, also, the steamer Caroline which was

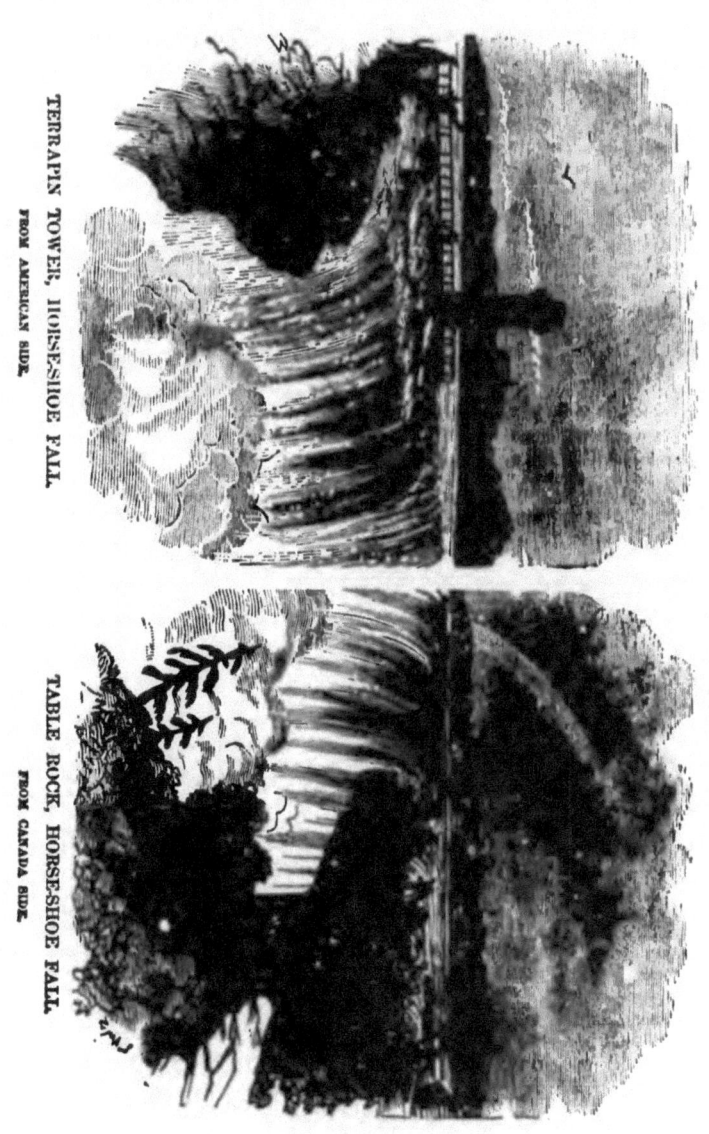

TERRAPIN TOWER, HORSE-SHOE FALL.
FROM AMERICAN SIDE.

TABLE ROCK, HORSE-SHOE FALL.
FROM CANADA SIDE.

conveying provisions and ammunition to the rebels, was cut adrift and sent afloat down the river, and over the Horse-Shoe Fall. Near the head of the Island the point may be seen where —before any bridges connected the Island with the mainland—Stedman, the occupier of the Island, crossed with his goats for pasture, hence the name Goat Island.

Fort Schlosser may be seen further up the river, also on the American side, where La Salle, the great explorer, first founded a trading post. This fort has changed hands, first from the French to the British, and next from the British to the Americans. About this spot the vessel, (named the *Griffin*,) which first navigated the river and lakes, was built. A Father Hannepin is said to have been the first white man who visited Niagara and saw the Falls, and who, like many who have succeeded him, published a very exaggerated account of them.

In wandering round Goat Island you have now reached the starting-point on it, viz., the Bridge at the Rapids, which you re-cross, and make direct for Point View.

POINT VIEW is situated close to the edge of the American Fall, and on the very brink of the precipice. From this point you get an excellent view of both Falls, but more particularly a distant view of the Horse-Shoe Fall. In the ferry-house at Point View there is a railway, down an incline of 1 in 31 feet. The cars are worked up and down by water power, and are completely under the control of those in charge. The fare for going up or down is 5 cents. At the bottom of the incline is the river, where boats may be hired to take you across to the Canada side of the river for 20 cents. Alongside of the railway incline, there are steps, up and down which parties may go free. The depth, to the edge of the water, is 260 feet—291 steps in all.

In the summer season a small steamer, called the "New Maid of the Mist," sails from the foot of the ferry stairs, up as near as possible to the base of the Horse-Shoe Fall. On proceeding on board you put on an oil-skin cloak and hood, which envelopes the whole person, excepting the face; and, thus clad, you stand on deck, viewing the Falls, as the steamer makes her speedy trip, and as she rocks about amid the agitated water. Certainly the view is excellent, unless when the sun is shining out very strong, then much of the sight is lost, owing to that and the spray from the Falls falling so thickly upon the face and eyes. The sail is one only of a few minutes, nevertheless we recommend all to take a trip on board the little craft. Great vigilance and care is necessary in steering round the base of the Fall. When it has reached the middle of the Fall the steam is shut off, and then the boat is swung round and carried down by the current, when steam is put on, and she is turned round to the landing-point, ready to take on

board another lot of passengers. Fare for the trip 50 cents, (2s. stg.).

In the ferry-house a beautifully clear stream of water, from the rock, is kept running continually, with tumblers provided for the use of visitors.

The Messrs. Porters, to whom the property belongs, have done much lately to improve the appearance of the place all around, and added greatly to the comfort and convenience of visitors, by providing seats, etc., etc.

Having spent some time at Point View, you may now proceed down the incline we have mentioned, cross the river in a small boat, and land on the Canadian side, near the Clifton House, on your road to a curiosity in its way—the Burning Springs—shown to strangers by an old native of Aberdeenshire, (Scotland).

Before reaching there, however, you will pass Table Rock—a view from off which will interest you.

TABLE ROCK, of which we give an illustration, is situated on the Canada side of the river, near the angle where the Horse-Shoe Fall pours over. It is a crag, which projects over the edge of the precipice, and is about 160 feet above the river. It is now much smaller than in former years, large portions having fallen away from it at different times. Near Table Rock there is another staircase, which you may descend and get a view from behind the great sheet of water which falls over the Horse Shoe, from off a narrow ledge of rock, called Termination Rock,* which, together with the ground all about it, shakes with the immense power of the water pouring down upon it. It is only, however, when the water is not very full, that this sight can be seen.

A favourite time with many for visiting the falls is at sunset, about which time some most beautiful phenomena are to be seen. Again, the view by moonlight is considered to be very fine, and presenting totally different features from any thing to be seen during the day. In winter time also, we understand, the Falls, together with the scenery around them, present sights well worth being seen by every tourist.

To reach Burning Springs it is a considerable walk round from the Clifton House, so that most parties engage a conveyance thither. The pedestrian, however, will enjoy the walk very much. The charge at the Burning Springs is 25 cents each.

BURNING SPRINGS.—From the sketch we give, readers at a distance will see an exact representation of where the Spring is exhibited, in an old wooden "shanty," pitch dark, but lighted up by the attendant, as he applies a light to the

---

* Since this was written, we understand that Termination Rock has been washed away—thus, we fear, depriving all in future of obtaining the view here alluded to.

THE BURNING SPRINGS, NIAGARA.

gas, as it issues up through an iron pipe fixed in a barrel, which is placed amidst the water 3 or 4 feet underneath. The water, which is charged with sulphurated hydrogen gas, rises in the rock close at hand, and forces its way up through the bed of the stream, which is there. Sometimes it burns much brighter than at other times, the water emitting a strong smell, similar to that of some mineral springs. When at Burning Springs, another and different view from any hitherto seen, is presented of the River Niagara, as it comes down from Lake Erie, and, in summer, the scenery in the neighbourhood of the Springs is beautiful in the extreme.

Leaving the Burning Springs, you may now proceed to the battle-ground of Lundy's Lane. There a wooden tower is erected, for the benefit of those who wish to ascend and obtain a magnificent view of the country. On the top of this tower one of the heroes of the Battle of Lundy's Lane will be met with, in the shape of an attendant, who will be glad to point out to you all the points of interest connected with the fighting between the Americans and the British, on those very fields you will there survey. If you happen to be a British visitor, the faithful attendant will not wound any national prejudices you may have regarding who was most successful on particular occasions during the struggle, but rather flatter them by leading you to understand that, of course, the British came off victorious. You will, however, perhaps, be in some doubt, after all, as to that, if you take the *ipse dixit* of this military chronicler, when you

learn that the American, who preceded or followed you on your visit, was parted company with on the same terms, and with an equally flattering account of how the Americans licked the British, and, of course, also won the battle! On the way to Lundy's Lane, you may pass through the pretty little village of Drummondville, named after General Drummond, commander of the British forces at the battle referred to. From Lundy's Lane you may now proceed on to the Suspension Bridge and the Whirlpool. Particulars respecting the Suspension Bridge will be found annexed, with illustrations of it.

The Whirlpool can be seen from the Canada side of the river. When at the Suspension Bridge you proceed along the top of the embankment, through fields and brushwood, following the course of the river, till its course turns at a right angle on towards Lake Ontario. It is at this angle of the river where the whirlpool is. An excellent view of the river and scenery along its banks, and around the whirlpool, is to be had from the Canada side immediately above it, and the beauty of the scene there may tempt you to prolong your rest on the wooden seat erected there for the wearied traveller.

The visitor who expects to see an immense whirlpool will, we think, be disappointed, as the Whirlpool, so called, consists of a series of eddies in the rapid stream as it reaches the end of the gorge at the angle of the river—more remarkable for being raised up in the centre of the

THE WHIRLPOOL—NIAGARA.

As stated on a previous page, the best view of the Whirlpool is to be had from the edge of the river, on the American side, and to give an idea of this scene we present an accurate representation of it, taken from the point of the angle, where the river, after proceeding to the point indicated in the far-off corner of the above sketch, whirls round, and finds its outlet down the river in the foreground, on its way to Lake Ontario. (See remarks on a previous page.)

THE BRIDGE LEADING TO BATH AND GOAT ISLANDS.

THE above sketch represents the well-known bridge which spans the river to Bath Island, and from thence leads across another small bridge to Goat Island. At Bath Island passengers pay the toll of 25 cents, which admit them to cross and recross during all the season. The bridge is not a suspension one, although similar to such in appearance. It is built on three piers, founded in the bed of the river by means of cribs filled with heavy masonry, and is altogether a graceful and substantial erection, strong enough for all the traffic passing across it, and for resisting the pow‐ current of the rapids as they rush down and flow under it on their way over the Ame..._..i Fall.

15

THE HORSE-SHOE FALL,

FROM BELOW.

To get the best idea of the magnitude of this fall is for the tourist to find his way down to the edge of the river, and get as close as possible to the fall. That can be accomplished easily by descending Biddle's stairs on Goat Island to the edge of the river, and thence by walking along the rocks until near enough to get a good view. The sensation experienced there, is much more thrilling than when viewing the fall from above.

RIVER NIAGARA, BELOW THE FALLS.

FROM THE CANADA SIDE.

ONE of the best views connected with the river is that presented in the above sketch, as it shows in bold outline the high, rocky, and precipitous embankment which lines both sides of the world's wonder. It is taken on the Canada side, from near where all which remains of Table Rock stands; giving an idea of the breadth of the river, the character of the roadway, with Clifton House in the distance.

16

THE AMERICAN FALL.

FROM THE CANADA SIDE.

THE best view of the American Fall is that to be seen from the point illustrated in the above sketch, being near the Clifton House, on the Canada side of the river. A portion of Goat Island is represented at the right-hand side, with the small fall between it, and what is termed Lunns Island, with the great American Fall in the centre, with Point View at the left-hand side, and the town of Niagara Falls forming the background. The river, a short way above the American Fall, glides rather smoothly but swiftly along, previous to taking its final leap over the fall.

NIAGARA—LOOKING TOWARDS LAKE ONTARIO.

FROM NEAR QUEENSTOWN HEIGHTS.

The scene represented above is considered one of the finest views which is to be found in the United States or Canada, embracing, as it does, such an extent and combination of landscape, river, and lake scenery. Below, rolls the mighty Niagara, appeased after its plunging and boiling career, now swiftly but silently pursuing its course to become engulphed in the placid waters of Lake Ontario, but only to join issue again with its gigantic neighbour, the St. Lawrence, and then travel in company together for 390 miles, carrying every other stream along with them—dashing down the rapids in their course, till joined by the beautiful Ottawa at a point near Montreal, when these three leviathans in the world of waters flow on gently towards Quebec, and there, joined by the St. Charles, afterwards find their exit, and become swallowed up in the " vasty deep."

BROCK'S MONUMENT, QUEENSTOWN HEIGHTS.

THE above is an exact representation of the monument erected to the British general, Sir Isaac Brock, who fell on Queenstown Heights in the memorable engagement fought there in the war of 1812. It is situated on the heights on the west bank of the River Niagara, and forms one of the first objects which arrests the attention of the tourist as he approaches Niagara per steamer on Lake Ontario; a rapid glance of which is also seen as the train proceeds between Niagara Town and Suspension Bridge. It should be visited by all tourists, if for no other reason than there to obtain one of the most magnificent views in the country. The landscape around the monument is varied and extensive—running over a highly-cultivated and fertile country, whilst the lake fronting to the north completes a picture at once grand and inspiring.

TRENTON FALLS, STATE OF NEW YORK.

THE tourist proceeding from New York, by the New York Central Railroad from Albany, on his way to Niagara, will find himself well paid by a visit to the Falls of Trenton, which are situated on the Utica and Black River Railroad, and 15 miles N. by E. of the Town of Utica, in the County of Oneida. Trenton Falls consist of a series of 6 falls, within the distance of two miles, with an aggregate fall of 312 feet, and present a sight more remarkable for the wild and romantic situation in which they are, than for their great volume of water.

The name of the stream on which these falls are, is known as West Canada Creek, which flows through a densely-wooded country—particularly near the falls—of which no sign is to be seen till the tourist comes upon them, at the edge of the gorge where they are situated, and down which the water rushes with great violence, as it comes from the falls, only to be lost to sight in the dark recesses of the wooded ravine. In one place, the height of the embankment is 140 feet, perpendicular.

At the upper falls the descent is 20 feet, from which the water rushes on to the second falls, called the Cascades. (See engraving.)

The third fall is named the Mill-dam, and, a little below, are the High Falls, which has a perpendicular fall of 109 feet. (See engraving.) Sherman's Falls—named so after Rev. Mr. Sherman, who lost his life there—form the fifth fall, with a descent of about 40 feet, until the last of this exquisite series of falls is reached, named Conrad's Falls.

18

THE HIGH FALLS, TRENTON FALLS.

THE CASCADES, TRENTON FALLS.

TRIP DOWN THE ST. LAWRENCE.

FROM NIAGARA FALLS TO MONTREAL AND QUEBEC,

Via the Lakes and Rapids.

Whilst other tours, in different parts of the United States and Canada, have their attractions — particularly, by railroad — and severally present sufficient inducements for a visit from the tourist; none, we believe, presents so great a variety of scenery—and that of the finest character, accompanied by comfortable locomotion and a few exciting incidents on the way—as are to be met with on the trip from Niagara to Montreal and Quebec *via* Lake Ontario—down the Rapids of the noble St. Lawrence—through the Thousand Islands, and the various other lakes, canals, etc., on the route.

This route may be taken either by steamer all the way from Lewiston or Niagara, or from there to Toronto, Kingston, Cape Vincent, or any of the other points of stoppage on the river hereafter stated; after visiting which, the tourist can embark on board the steamer again at any of the stopping places, and proceed on his journey.

To render this trip as intelligible as possible, we propose placing the names of each place of interest, on both sides of the river, in such order that the stranger will at once be able to know on which side each town is situated. This will be seen at once by making a division in the page, representing the channel of the river, with the towns, rapids, lakes and canals placed in their relative positions; so that, with the distances and routes given elsewhere, we hope to render such information as will be useful and interesting to the reader. We shall take LEWISTON as the starting point.

ROUTE FROM LEWISTON (NIAGARA) TO QUEBEC.

TOWNS AND STOPPING-PLACES.

CANADIAN, OR NORTH BANK OF RIVER.

QUEENSTOWN, a village situated nearly opposite to Lewiston. Its chief objects of attraction are the handsome Suspension Bridge, with Brock's Monument, situated on the heights, from which a most magnificent view of the lake and the surrounding country is obtained.

AMERICAN, OR SOUTH BANK OF RIVER.

LEWISTON is the point from which the steamer starts—being at the head of river navigation—about 7 miles from Niagara Falls, and 7 miles from the mouth of the river, whence it falls into the lake. The Buffalo, Niagara Falls and Lewiston Railroad terminates at this place.

LAKE ONTARIO.

THIS is the smallest and most easterly of the five great lakes which communicate with the St. Lawrence, and divides the State of New York from Canada, on the north. It is 190 miles long, and its greatest breadth 55 miles. Its greatest depth is 600 feet, and it is navigable in every part for the largest-sized ships. It is never entirely closed with ice, and rarely freezes, even in the coldest weather, except in shallow places along the shore. In summer time, a sail upon this lake is delightful, especially to the angler, who, if he chooses to cast his lines into its usually placid waters, will find no dearth of fish, which abound here in great variety. On either side of the lake are seen numerous towns and villages, several of which are of considerable business importance. We append brief notices of the most noted of these places.

CANADIAN SIDE.

In proceeding along the north, or Canadian, side of the lake, the first point touched is

AMERICAN SIDE.

The first stopping-place on the American, or south, side of the Lake is YOUNGSTOWN, 6 miles below, and 1 mile

21

curve of the viaduct, resting on piers of solid masonry, over which the Grand Trunk Railway is carried, tends to enhance the picturesqueness of the view. The town is surrounded by a rich agricultural district, diversified by hill and dale, wood and stream; the evidence of which is the number of wagons—crammed with quarters of fat beef, mutton and pork, turkeys, chickens, eggs, butter, vegetables and fish—to be seen crowding the Town Hall Square on Saturdays.

The lumber trade carried on at this port is also very extensive. Population about 8,000.

COBURG, 8 miles below Port Hope, is the terminus of the Coburg and Peterborough Railroad. It has a good harbour, and does an extensive shipping business with Rochester, and other cities on the opposite side of the lake. Victoria College, established by act of the Provincial Legislature, in 1842, is in this town. It also contains the most extensive cloth manufactories in the Province. There are also iron, marble and leather manufactories, with a number of breweries and distilleries, 9 good hotels, and 60 or 70 substantial stores. Population about 6,000.

COLBORNE, 14 miles below Coburg, is a flourishing town, having a fine back country, whose produce finds quick sales in its markets. It has a good landing for steamers, many of which touch here on their passages up and down the lake.

A good business is done in this town in curing white-fish and salmon-trout, which abound in the lake, and are taken in great quantities. A stage-route is established between this place and Norwood, 32 miles distance. Fare, $2.

Leaving Colborne, the steamer soon reaches the widest part of the lake, and, running a distance of some 25 miles, passes *Nicholas Point* and *Island*, *Wicked Point*, and *Point Peter*, on the latter of which is a fine light-house. This light is a conspicuous object to mariners, who, when off Prince Edward's, the main-land, experience the full force of easterly and westerly winds.

DUCK ISLAND, which is attached to Canada, is another noted object for the mariner, either ascending or descending the

place, to Rochester proper, there are a succession of falls and rapids, some of the former being very grand and imposing. The falls at Carthage are 75 feet, one a little further up is 20 feet, and the great falls—within the city, a few feet from the Central Railroad Bridge—is 96 feet. It was at these latter falls that the once famous Sam Patch made his last leap, by which he lost his life. He commenced his singular career by plunging from the Pawtucket Falls, in Rhode Island, and afterwards continued to jump from all the high bridges, and other elevated points in the country, including Niagara, without meeting an accident. It is supposed that he was intoxicated at the time he made his last jump, and hence lost his balance during his descent, and struck the water horizontally, which must have knocked the breath entirely out of his body, as he was not seen to rise after striking the water, although 10,000 spectators were anxiously looking for his appearance. His dead body was found some miles below the falls.

Further up the river, near the town of Portage, N. Y., there are three beautiful falls, respectively, 60, 90 and 110 feet, all within the space of 2 miles, each differing in character, and each having peculiar attractions. But more wonderful, than the falls, are the stupendous walls of the river, which rise almost perpendicularly, to a height of 400 feet, and extend along the stream, for 3 miles, with almost as much regularity and symmetry as if constructed by art.

Leaving the mouth of the Genesee, the steamer passes the small town of *Pultneyville*, and some other lesser settlements, and reaches the mouth of

GREAT SODUS BAY, which is 5 miles long and 3 miles in breadth, and makes an excellent, safe harbour, the entrance of which is protected by substantial piers, built by the United States.

SODUS POINT is a small town, and port of entry, situated at the mouth of Sodus Bay.

LITTLE SODUS BAY, 14 miles below Great Sodus, is another good anchorage ground, for vessels to ride, in times of severe weather.

OSWEGO is on both sides of Oswego

carrying passengers and produce which come from inland by the Rideau Canal, and from the Bay of Quinte, to the different ports on the lake.

There are several mineral springs in Kingston, which have attained some celebrity for their medical properties. One of these, situated near the Penitentiary, is said to resemble the celebrated Cheltenham Springs, in England. Another, whose waters are unusually strong, and, by analyzation, have been found to contain valuable medical virtues, has been likened to the Artesian Well at St. Catherine's.

gives, however, great water power, and its banks are covered with prosperous towns and villages.

CHAUMONT BAY, just above Black River, abounds in a variety of fine fish, large quantities of which are taken by established fisheries.

CAPE ST. VINCENT is nearly opposite Grand or Wolf Island, and is the northern terminus of the Watertown and Rome Railroad. In the warm months, this place is much resorted to by fishing and pleasure parties, being contiguous to the "Thousand Islands."

THE THOUSAND ISLANDS.

THESE Islands, which have obtained a world-wide celebrity, consist of fully 1800 islands, of all sizes and shapes—from a few yards long, to several miles in length; some, presenting little or nothing but bare masses of rock, whilst others are so thickly wooded over, that nothing but the most gorgeous green foliage (in summer) is to be seen; whilst, in autumn, the leaves present colours of different hues of light crimson, yellow, purple and other colours scarcely imaginable, and yet more difficult to describe.

The tourist who is fond of practising the "gentle art," will find any quantity he is able and willing to fish for—the river abounding in fish of the most marvellous quantity and size. The angler will find plenty of excellent accommodation at Clayton or Alexandria Bay, with boats, etc. To enjoy a day or two amongst the Thousand Islands to the most advantage, is for the tourist to take up his quarters for a few days at either of these places, and sail amongst the islands with a row-boat. The tourist who is acquainted with the islands on "Lomond's Silver Loch," opposite Luss, in the Highlands of Scotland, will have some idea of what the Thousand Islands are—only that the latter extend fully 50 miles along the channel of the St. Lawrence, with some of the islands of much larger dimensions than those either on Loch Lomond or Loch Katrine. Names are given to some of the islands, whilst several have light-houses erected upon them.

With these remarks, we will now proceed, as if on board the American steamer, down the American channel, through them—there being one channel for the Canadian Company's boats, and another for the American Company's.

Leaving Kingston, the tourist in the Canadian Company's steamer will proceed on for six miles, and enter the regions of the Thousand Islands. For a description of the scenery of the route, we quote from a writer who thus describes it:

"These islands appear so thickly studded, that the appearance to the spectator, on approaching them, is as if the vessel steered her course towards the head of a landlocked bay which barred all further progress. Coming nearer, a small break in the line of shore opens up, and he enters between what he now discovers to be islands, and islands which are innumerable. Now, he sails in a wide channel be-

Leaving CAPE VINCENT, the steamer now proceeds towards the islands, and, after winding her course amongst them for about twenty miles, reaches the stopping-place called

CLAYTON, a small, well-built village, from which a considerable lumber trade is carried on, several rafts of which may probably be seen in French Creek, close at hand, ready for being "run" down the St. Lawrence to Montreal or Quebec. Several of the finest steamers which navigate the St. Lawrence were built here.

ALEXANDRIA BAY, 12 miles from Clayton, is soon reached—in approaching which, the tourist will admire the exquisite

25

THE THOUSAND ISLANDS, ON THE ST. LAWRENCE.

FROM A PHOTOGRAPH TAKEN AT BROCKVILLE, C. W.

tween more distant shores; again, he enters into a strait so narrow that the large paddle-boxes of the steamer almost sweep the foliage, on either side, as she pursues her devious course. Now, the islands are miles in circumference; and again, he passes some which are very small, shaded by a single tiny tree occupying the handful of earth which represents the 'dry land.' On all, the trees grow to the water's edge, and dip their outer branches in the clear blue lake. Sometimes the *mirage* throws its air of enchantment on the whole, and the more distant islands seem floating in mid-heaven—only descending into the lake as a nearer approach dispels the illusion, and when the rushing steamer breaks the fair surface of the water in which all this loveliness is reflected, as in a mirror."

BROCKVILLE (Canada West) is the county town for the united counties of Leeds and Grenville. A steamer plies to Norristown, on the American side. All the American as well as Canadian steamers touch here. The tourist cannot fail to admire the fine location of Brockville, and its numerous tastefully laid out gardens, stretching down to the river's edge, as well as some neat built villas on the banks. Named after Gen. Brock, whose monument, at Queenstown Heights, commemorates his fall in battle there in 1812. Distant from Kingston 48 miles by rail, and Montreal 125 miles. The steamer, after leaving Brockville, proceeds for 12 miles, and reaches the town of

PRESCOTT, which is situated almost immediately opposite to Ogdensburg. At Prescott, both lines of steamers touch. From there, branches off the railroad to OTTAWA CITY—the future capital of Canada—a visit to which will well repay the tourist. 55 miles to Ottawa per railroad. Considerable amount of business is done with Ogdensburg, opposite, to and from which plies two ferry steamers. Population about 4,000. 113 miles from Montreal by rail.

One mile below Prescott is "Windmill Point," being the ruins of an old windmill, where, in 1837, the Canadian patriots, under a Polish exile named Von Shultz, established their headquarters, but were subsequently driven from it, with great loss.

scenery which now opens up to view on every turn which the steamer takes. From Alexandria Bay, some of the finest views of the islands, to our mind, are to be seen; whilst from the high points near the village, upwards of one hundred of the islands can be counted in one view. The situation of Alexandria Bay must always render it a favourite place with the tourist who delights in romantic situations or good sport. After steaming along for other 22 miles, the last of the Thousand Islands is seen, and the steamer touches on the Canadian side, at the thriving and prettily situated town of Brockville (Canada West).

MORRISTOWN is situated exactly opposite Brockville, with which it is connected by steam ferry every half hour, 1 mile distance.

The American steamer, after leaving Brockville, proceeds on to

OGDENSBURG, now an important link in the chain of communication between the United States and Canada, with a railroad to Lake Champlain, (118 miles off) and which also connects at Rouse's Point with the other lines, to Boston and New York, as well as to Montreal. A considerable trade is done at Ogdensburg, whilst the situation of the town is one of the prettiest on the whole route. Settled by the French in 1748, attacked by the Mohawk Indians in 1749, and, on the defeat of Montcalm at Quebec, the settlement was abandoned by the French.

After Ogdensburg, comes Waddington, opposite to Ogden Island. Thirty miles further on is Louisville, from which stages run to Messina Springs, 7 miles distant.

The American steamer proceeds onwards to the first rapid in the route, known by the name of Gallop's Rapids, succeeded by others of lesser note. (See Descent of the Rapids.)

Four miles further on is Chimney Island, on which stands the ruin of an old French fortification. A short distance from there is CHRYSELLER'S FARM, where a battle was fought between the Americans and the British, in 1813, at the time when the Americans, under Gen. Wilkinson, were descending the river to attack Montreal, but which attempt was afterwards abandoned.

DESCENT OF THE RAPIDS.

AT LONG SAULT.

These Rapids, universally allowed to be the most extensive and the most exciting to be found on this continent, extend in continuous lines for a distance of nine miles—the stream being divided near its centre by an island. The channels on both sides are descended with safety, although steamers usually pass on the south side, which is a trifle narrower than the other. The current moves along this channel with astonishing velocity, drifting rafts at the rate of 12 or 14 miles an hour, the waters alone moving at least 20 miles an hour. It needs not the aid of wind or steam to descend these swift-sweeping waters, and hence when vessels enter the current they shut off steam, and trust to the guidance of the helm only as they are borne on their rapid voyage by the force of the stream alone. Nature presents but few sights more grand and beautiful than is presented from the deck of a steamer when descending these rapids. The unequal movement of the waves, as they plunge from one eddy to another, causes the boat to rise and fall with a motion not unlike that experienced on the ocean after a gale of wind has disturbed its bosom. The constant roar of the waters as they dash and leap along their furious course, filling the atmosphere with misty foam; the wild and tumultuous force with which wave struggles with wave to reach the depths below; the whirlings of the yawning eddies, that seem strong and angry enough to engulph any and every thing that ventures within their embrace, and the ever-changing features, form and course of the writhing, restless stream, all unite in presenting a scene of surpassing grandeur.

The navigation of these rapids, although generally conducted with entire safety, requires, nevertheless, great nerve, force and presence of mind on the part of the pilots—generally Indians—who essay to guide the staggering steamer on its course. It is imperative that the vessel should keep her head straight with the stream, for if she diverges in the least, so as to present her side to the current, she would be in-

ROUTE FROM PRESCOTT.

DOWN THE RAPIDS.

The steamer, after leaving Prescott, proceeds, passing, on its way, between Chimney Island and Drummond's Island —now steering for Tick Island, thence northwest round the western end of Isle aux Galops, and by Fraser's Island to a point opposite Lock 27 of the canal, which extends from the beginning of the Gallop Rapids to Point Iroquois and rapids. Instead of passing through that canal, however, the steamer proceeds down the Gallop Rapids.

GALLOP RAPIDS.

In sailing down these rapids, the steamer passes on its way Isle aux Galops, and several other small islands in the channel, onwards to Long Point—passing down the rapids between Tousson's Island and the south bank of the river; thence on again, and down the Iroquois Rapids, shortly after passing which we reach Ogden's Island, with rapids on each side of it. (At this point the *up* steamers ascend *via* the Rapide Platte Canal, from Lock 23 to 24.) After passing Ogden's Island, and several smaller ones, we pass Goose Neck Island and Crysler's Island, and proceed on between the two Cat Islands, the Upper Long Sault—now called Croyle's Island—and the rapids on the north-western end of it, at Farren's Point, where there is a short canal for the *up* steamer to pass through.

LONG SAULT RAPIDS.

Sailing down the rapid there, we pass at some distance Dickenson's Landing, close to Long Sault Island, and prepare to what is termed "shoot the Rapids of the Long Sault"—passing by the north channel, and downward through the rapids between Sheek's Island and Barnhart's Island. After steaming a short distance, with smooth sailing, we again reach rapids, being those between the town of Cornwall and Cornwall Island. (The *up* steamers enter in at Lock 15, at Cornwall, and passing along the canal with its eight locks, find an exit at Lock 22.) For a description of the passage

STEAMERS DESCENDING LOST CHANNEL, LONG SAULT RAPIDS, ST. LAWRENCE,
WITH STEAMER ASCENDING THE RIVER, VIA CANAL.

stantly capsized and lost. In order to prevent such catastrophies, boats traversing the rapids have their rudders constructed in such a manner that any amount of power can be brought to bear upon them at any moment. Not only is the wheel guided by strongly-wrought, but pliable chains, which are managed from a position near the bows, but a strong tiller is adjusted at the stern, which requires the aid of four powerful men, while two are working at the wheel, to keep the vessel's head in its proper direction.

The greatest danger attends the adventurous raftsmen, whose skill, courage and physical strength are perhaps not excelled by any similar body of men in the world. But, despite all these advantages, many a raft has been broken, and many a gallant raftsman's life has been lost upon this remorseless tide of waters.

ST. LAWRENCE.

down the Long Sault Rapids, see the opposite column on this page. For illustration of the same, see engraving.

St. Regis is an old Indian village, one of the historical incidents connected with which, is a marauding excursion made by the St. Regis Indians, into Massachusetts, to recover a bell for their church, which, having been captured on its way to Canada from France, was purchased for the church of Deerfield, Massachusetts—but retaken from there by the said Indians, who claimed it as theirs, and who murdered, in the dead of night, 47, and captured 112, of the unsuspecting and innocent citizens of Deerfield. Having obtained the bell, they carried it, suspended from a pole, on their shoulders, for 150 miles, and it now hangs in the Catholic Church of St. Regis, built about 160 years ago.

OF THE

Steamers in their passage *up* the St. Lawrence, when they come to the rapids, pass round them, by entering the stupendous canals which have been made for the purpose of enabling them to pass *up*, as well as *down*, the river—although it is in the passage *down* the river, such as we are now describing, in which all the beauty and enjoyment of the trip is to be seen and realized. Having passed through the most exciting part of the whole trip, we now arrive at the town of Cornwall, at the foot of the Long Sault Rapids—on the Canada side.

CORNWALL is the boundary line between the United States and Canada, so that, after this point, all the points of interest remaining are now within the British possessions. Here the Cornwall Canal may be seen, 12 miles long, by which vessels pass up—as already mentioned.

LAKE ST. FRANCIS.

AFTER leaving Cornwall, we proceed on, passing St. Regis Island, situated in mid-channel, until we enter Lake St. Francis, passing between the Squaw's Island and Butternut Islands, with lighthouse to the north, in Lancaster Shoal. The steamer now steers close to the floating light, onwards to Cherry Island Light, and passing McGee's Point Light, on the main land, (north shore,) sails on towards the Rapids of Coteau du Lac.

COTEAU RAPIDS AND CEDARS RAPIDS.

AT the COTEAU DU LAC RAPIDS, a cluster of sixteen islands interrupt the regular navigation, but through which the skilful pilot steers first down the rapid between the main land and Giron Island, thence down again between French Island, and Maple and Thorn Islands, and again between Prisoner's Island and Broad Island,

CHANNEL

COTEAU DU LAC "is a small village, situated at the foot of Lake St. Francis. The name, as well as the style of the buildings, denotes its French origin. Just below the village are the Coteau Rapids."

CEDARS RAPIDS are situated between the village of Cedars (north shore) and village of St. Timothé, (south shore,) with 8 or 10

and emerging into smooth water along-side of Grand Island, until, shortly after, the Cedars Rapids are reached.

CEDARS.—This village presents the same marks of French origin as Coteau du Lac. In the expedition of Gen. Amherst, a detachment of three hundred men, that were sent to attack Montreal, were lost in the rapids near this place. "The passage through these rapids is very exciting. There is a peculiar motion of the vessel, which, in descending, seems like settling down, as she glides from one ledge to another. In passing the rapids of the Split Rock, a person, unacquainted with the navigation of these rapids, will almost involuntarily hold his breath until this ledge of rocks, which is distinctly seen from the deck of the steamer, is passed. At one time the vessel seems to be running directly upon it, and you feel certain that she will strike; but a skilful hand is at the helm, and in an instant more it is passed in safety."

small islands in the channel where the rapids are.

On the south side of the river is Beau-harnois.

BEAUHARNOIS "is a small village at the foot of the Cascades, on the south bank of the river. (Here r vessels enter the Beau-harnois Canal—with nine locks—and pass around the rapids of the Cascades, Cedars and Coteau, into Lake St. Francis, a distance of 14 miles.) On the north bank, a branch of the Ottawa enters into the St. Lawrence." *

After passing down the rapids at Cedars, the steamer again enters the smooth waters of the St. Lawrence, only, however, to be soon once more broken in upon by the Cascade Rapids.

THE CASCADE RAPIDS AND LAKE ST. LOUIS.

THE CASCADE RAPIDS are situated between Cascade's Point and Buisson Pointe, in which are situated Mary's Reef, Dog's Reef, Split Rock, Round Island and Isle aux Cascades. On the north side of these rapids, the majestic river Ottawa comes sweeping along, and round both sides of Isle Perrot, and here joins issue with the St. Lawrence, in Lake St. Louis. A smooth and pleasant sail of 24 miles along Lake St. Louis will be enjoyed, until the last rapids of all are reached, viz., Lachine.

The steamboat track proceeds through Lake St. Louis, passing three floating light-ships and the town of Lachine, on north bank, and Caughnawaga, on south bank of river.

LA CHINE.—This village is nine miles from Montreal, with which it is connected by railroad. "The La Chine Rapids begin just below the town. The current is here so swift and wild, that to avoid it a canal has been cut around these rapids. This canal is a stupendous work, and reflects much credit upon the energy and enterprise of the people of Montreal.

At La Chine is the residence of Sir George Simpson, Governor of the Hudson's Bay Company, and of the officers of this, the chief post of that corporation. It is from this point that the orders from head-quarters in London are sent to all the many posts throughout the vast territory of the company; and near the end of April

CAUGHNAWAGA.—"This is an Indian village, lying on the south bank of the river, near the entrance of the La Chine Rapids. It derived its name from the Indians that had been converted by the Jesuits, who were called "Caughnawagas," or "praying Indians." This was probably a misnomer, for they were distinguished for their predatory incursions upon their neighbours in the New England provinces. The Indians at Caughnawaga subsist chiefly by navigating barges and rafts down to Montreal, and, in winter, by a trade in moccasins, snow-shoes, etc. They are mostly Roman Catholics, and possess an elegant church."

Many of the Caughnawaga Indians are

RAFTS OF LUMBER "RUNNING" THE RAPIDS, AT CEDARS, ON THE ST. LAWRENCE.

MONTREAL TO QUEBEC.

THE tourist who is desirous of proceeding on his voyage at once, only staying until after he has visited the commercial capital of Canada, and enjoyed the magnificent view from the mountain behind the City of Montreal, or from off the top of the Notre Dame in Place d'Armes, will find the Quebec steamers—comfortably fitted up and well appointed—ready to start every evening about six o'clock. From the fact of the steamers sailing both from Montreal and Quebec in the evening, a short time during daylight is only left for the traveller to see much of the river and its banks between these two cities. This need hardly be regretted, however, so much, as the scenery, for the most part, is tame and uninteresting —the chief attractions being the neat and picturesquely-situated French-Canadian villages, which are situated on its banks, here and there, the tin-covered spires of their churches in the clear moonlight night—the sailing of the steamer swiftly down the stream, and the beautiful moonlight on a still summer's night—all contribute to render such a trip pleasant, and a change from what is almost nowhere else to be enjoyed in any other trip which can be taken in Canada.

Leaving Montreal, therefore, by the steamer, a good view of the city and St. Helen's Island—in the middle of the stream—is to be seen. The island is fortified, and commands the passage of the river.

The RAPIDS OF ST. MARY are just below St. Helen's Island, and, although not dangerous, are very troublesome to the river craft, which are much retarded in their movements by these obstinate rapids.

The first village passed is that of Longueil—three miles below Montreal, on south side of the river—the terminus of the Grand Trunk Railroad to Portland and Quebec.

LONGUE POINT AND POINT AUX TREMBLES, on the Island of Montreal, are successively passed on the left, and BOUCHERVILLE on the opposite shore.

The ISLAND OF ST. THERESA is 15 miles below the city, and near the mouth of Ottawa River.

VARENNES, on the south-east side of the river, is a beautiful village, which is often resorted to on account of the mineral springs to be found in its vicinity.

WILLIAM HENRY, or SOREL, 30 miles below Varennes, is a town of some 3000 inhabitants. It stands on the site of an old fort built in 1665, at the mouth of Richelieu River, and the first permanent settlement was made in 1685. The "fort" was taken, and occupied in May, 1776, by a party of Americans, in their retreat from Quebec, on the death of Gen. Montgomery.

Leaving *Richelieu River*, which is the outlet of Lake Champlain into the St. Lawrence, we pass a succession of small islands, and enter

LAKE ST. PETER'S.

THIS lake, which is formed by an expansion of the river, is about twenty-five miles long and nine miles broad, but is, for the most part, rather shallow. Recent improvements, however, have rendered the navigation such that the largest sailing vessels, and the Canadian and Liverpool steamers now pass up during the summer season to Montreal. Like all the other lakes, that of St. Peter's assumes a very different appearance in the summer season, during mild weather, from what it does during a gale of wind. Then it presents all the appearance, as well as the dangers of the sea, and rafts on their way down the river are frequently wrecked on its waters—the violence of the winds and waves being such as to render the rafts unmanageable, and part them asunder, to the loss sometimes of life as well as the timber.

On the south bank of the river is the small village of Port St. Francis, 82 miles from Montreal.

OTTAWA, CANADA WEST.

THE notoriety which this city, in embryo, has received lately, first as being fixed upon as the seat of government for Canada, and then decided against as such by the provincial legislature,—although it had been acquiesced in by Her Majesty as the most advisable locality—has invested it with a significance which, otherwise, it would not, in all probability, have obtained.

Ottawa is the new name given to the town of Bytown, by which it has long been known, as the centre of the immense lumber district of the River Ottawa. It is situated on that river, where the Rivers Ridea and Gatineau, and the Rideau Canal, all meet.

The town is intersected by the Rideau Canal and bridge, and forms three districts, viz.: that of Lower Town, on the east; Central Town, on the west; and Upper Town, on the north-west; all of which, however, are on the south side of the River Ottawa, and in Canada West, the River Ottawa, as is well known, forming the boundary line between Canada East and Canada West. The town was laid out under the command of Colonel By of the Royal Engineers, who constructed, also, the Rideau Canal. Hence the original name of the town being called Bytown—although now called Ottawa, after the magnificent river on which it stands.

The streets are all wide and regularly laid out, and, so far, reflects great credit on the engineering skill employed. Lower Town is the most important portion of the town, and, in all probability, will become the chief business part, as the population and business increases. The two principal streets of Lower Town are Rideau street and Sussex street. In Rideau street there are several substantial, stone-built stores and dwellings. In Sussex street there are also a few; the majority, however, are wooden erections, both old and new. In Central Town the buildings are almost all of stone, presenting one excellent street, called Spark street; whilst Upper Town exhibits a mixture of both stone and wooden buildings in its Wellington street. All the buildings in the town are exceedingly plain, but substantially built, and, being built of gray limestone, resemble very much in appearance some of the streets of Montreal, as well as in the granite city of Aberdeen (Scotland). On "Barrack Hill," the highest elevation of the town, are situated what are termed the government buildings—the remains, however, we should say, rather than of actual buildings. There are a few small out-houses and offices—which certainly do not deserve the name of government buildings—with sundry small cannon, taking their ease on the ground alongside of carriages, which have evidently seen service of some sort. These are the "dogs of war," which are intended, we presume, to protect the town against all invaders. On Barrack Hill is, however, also the residence of the chief military authority of the place. The "location" of these buildings and the "gun battery" alluded to, is certainly one of the finest we have seen any where, either in Canada or the United States—equal, in some respects, even to the famous citadel of Quebec. In the rear is Central Town, whilst Upper and Lower Town are completely commanded by it on each side, whilst in front is a precipitous embankment running down, almost perpendicular, to the river, several hundred feet, thus completely sweeping the river and opposite shore, north, east, and west; so that, in a military point of view, Ottawa certainly occupies one of the finest natural positions any where in Canada; and, in that respect, is the key to an immense territory of back country, valuable for its wood and minerals.

The stranger, on visiting Ottawa for the first time, is apt to be disappointed that he does not find a larger "city," and one more advanced, in many respects; but it must be recollected that it has been forced into public notice from the cause we have already alluded to, and obtained a publicity, with which parties at a distance are apt to connect wrong or exaggerated ideas; and if the town is not larger than it is, the fault rests as much in the imaginations of individuals, as with the inhabitants, generally, of the town itself, who, in the short time, since Bytown became a place of note, have been doing their utmost to make it "go a-head." In the desire to do so, however, some of the landholders there, we fear, by putting very high prices on their lots, and landlords refusing to give

OTTAWA, CANADA WEST.—UPPER TOWN, LOOKING WEST.

CHAUDIERE FALLS—RIDEAU FALLS, ETC.

leases at reasonable rates, have only tended to defeat the very object which they, and all the inhabitants ought to have in view, viz., giving every facility in their power, and offering every inducement they can, for parties at a distance to locate amongst them. In fact, the idea that Ottawa was selected as the headquarters of the government, has had any thing but a beneficial effect so far, in some respects, upon the town; but there is the consolation, that whether it is to be the seat of government or not, there is no doubt, that of necessity, it is destined to become—it may be gradually—the centre of a much more extensive trade, a town of much greater importance than it is at present, and the point, round which radiate a number of other towns, and extensive agricultural districts, of which Ottawa is the capital and centre, and, in all human probability, always likely to remain so. From it, a large wholesale and retail trade is, and must always, be done—with the districts round about; whilst, as is well known, it is the centre of a district, which, for extensive forests of fine lumber, has no superior in America.

The scenery around Ottawa is far beyond what we had any idea of, and the view from the Barrack Hill, is one of surpassing grandeur and extent, combining in it a trinity of river, landscape, and fall scenery, which few places can boast of.

Looking to the west—(see engraving)—at the west end of the town are situated, the celebrated Chaudière Falls, which fall about 40 feet, and the spray of which may be seen a long way off, ascending in the air.

In the early part of the season, (say in May,) these falls are not seen to so much advantage, the river then being, generally, so much swollen with the immense volume of water from the upper lakes and the tributaries of the Ottawa. Then they partake, in some respects, more of the character of huge rapids. Farther on in the season, however, they appear more in their real character of "falls," and are a sight worth seeing, although they are being very much encroached upon, by lumber establishments. An excellent view of the falls, as well as of the rapids, is got from off the suspension bridge, which crosses the river quite close to them. At the eastern suburb of Ottawa, again, called New Edinburgh, there is a little Niagara, in miniature, in the Rideau Falls, and one of the prettiest little falls to be seen any where. Although only of 30 feet fall, they present features of interest and great beauty.

The town of Ottawa is supplied, in many parts, with gas. Its markets afford an excellent supply of cheap provisions, whilst the purity of the air, from its elevated position, renders it one of the healthiest towns in Canada.

Emigrants, in looking to Ottawa, will do well to remember, that it is only the agricultural labourer, or farmer with capital, to whom its locality offers inducements at present.

Amongst the schemes for connecting Canada East with the Western States, is the Ottawa Ship Canal, via the Ottawa and French Rivers to Lake Huron, which, if successful in being established, will render Ottawa, more than ever, one of the great entrepots of that route and traffic.

The communication between Ottawa and Montreal, is by rail via Prescott; also by river, per steamer to Grenville, rail from Grenville to Carrillon; thence, steamer to Lachine; thence, rail to Montreal. To Canada West, on the St. Lawrence, via rail. To Ogdensburg, via rail to Prescott, and steamer across the St. Lawrence. Distances:—from Montreal, 126 miles; Quebec, 296 miles; Toronto, 223 miles; Kingston, 95 miles; Prescott, 55 miles; New York, 450 miles; Boston, 485 miles. Population, about 12,000.

For the information of emigrants proceeding to the newly-opened districts, where free lands are to be had, full information regarding these, with routes and fares, will be found in another portion of this work.

The views of Upper Town, and Lower and Central Town, as given elsewhere, are from pencil drawings made for this work, by Mr. Eastman, artist, of Ottawa. All who know Ottawa will be able to attest to the very faithful manner in which they are done, and that the engravers have preserved all the truthfulness in detail, in enabling us to present, for the first time, we believe, complete and accurate views of Ottawa, Canada West.

MONTREAL TO OTTAWA, C. W.

THIS beautiful route may be traversed either by rail from Montreal to Prescott Junction, and thence by rail to Ottawa, as described elsewhere; or it may be taken by way of rail to Lachine, steamer fr..m Lachine to Carrillon, rail from Carrillon to Grenville, and Grenville to Ottawa by steamer again. By this route it will be seen that there are several changes to be made, which cannot be avoided, on account of the rapids on the river, which cannot be "run" by the steamer.

This route is one so little known, that, notwithstanding the disadvantages which changing so often presents, we have thought it advisable to give a brief account of the trip to Ottawa, as made by us last June, addressing ourselves as if the reader were going. Proceeding in cab or omnibus to Griffintown — 1¼ miles from post-office, Montreal — you arrive and book at the Lachine Railroad Depot; fare through to Ottawa, first class, $3; second class, $2. Strange to say, no baggage is "checked through," on this route as via Grand Trunk railroad, or the other lines in the United States.

Started on the cars, therefore, with a string of tickets to and from the different points on your way, you soon reach Lachine, nine miles off. At Lachine you change cars, and step on board the steamer "Lady Simpson" in waiting, and once under weigh, you get a fine view of the mighty St. Lawrence, with Lake St. Louis close at hand.

Not long after the steamer starts, breakfast will be announced, which may be partaken of, if you had not got it before you started from Montreal. An excellent breakfast for 1s. 10½d. currency, (1s. 6d. stg.,) or 37½ cents. If a fine morning, you will be delighted with the sail, as the steamer skims along the shore of the Island of Montreal, till she reaches St. Anne's, at the extreme corner of that island. At St. Anne's, the steamer leaves the St. Lawrence, and passes through the locks there, and is then on the bosom of the Ottawa. You will scarcely be able to imagine it to be a river; in reality, it forms the Lake of the Two Mountains, being one of the numerous lakes which the Ottawa may be said to be a succession of.

At St. Anne's you will get an excellent view of the substantial stone bridge of the Grand Trunk Railway, which here crosses the Ottawa, and which forms a striking contrast to the mistaken policy of the railway companies in the United States in building so many "rickety" wooden bridges—with their warnings up of fines of so much if you trot a horse over them—and which in going over so many accidents have occurred. Here, possibly, you may observe, against one of the piers of this bridge, a portion of a large raft, which, in "running" the rapids last season, became unmanageable and dashed up against the bridge —scattering the raft in all directions—to the great loss of the proprietor of it. Some of the logs may be seen yet, resting up against the pier of the bridge, as if trying to clear all before them, and the gigantic pier standing up, in its mighty strength, as if bidding them float quietly past.

St. Anne's is the spot where the poet Moore located the scene of his celebrated Canadian Boat Song.

CANADIAN BOAT SONG.
BY THOMAS MOORE.

Faintly as tolls the evening chime,
Our voices keep tune and our oars keep time;
Soon as the woods on shore look dim,
We'll sing at St. Anne's our parting hymn.
    Row, brothers, row, the stream runs fast,
    T..e Rapids are near, and the daylight's past.

Why should we yet our sail unfurl?
There is not a breath the blue wave to curl;
But when the wind blows off the shore,
Oh! sweetly we'll rest our weary oar.
    Blow, breezes, blow, the stream runs fast,
    The Rapids are near, and the daylight's past.

Ottawa's tide ! this trembling moon
Shalt see us float over thy surges soon.
Saint of this green isle ! hear our prayers,
Oh ! grant us cool heavens and favoring airs.
Blow, breezes, blow, the stream runs fast,
The Rapids are near, and the daylight 's past.

Started from St. Anne's you shortly reach a beautiful expansion of the Ottawa—which forms here what is called THE LAKE OF THE TWO MOUNTAINS—named from the two mountains which are seen to the north, rising four hundred to five hundred feet high.

After sailing a short time, and with your face to the bow of the steamer, you will observe, to the right, where this great river—coming slowly and silently along—is divided by the Island of Montreal ; the one fork of the river which you observe to the north-east, winding its way past the island, after which it makes its acquaintance with the St. Lawrence, to the north-east of Montreal. The other fork, or division on which you have just started from, at St. Anne's, meets the St. Lawrence there ; although, strange to say, the waters of these two immense rivers—as if not relishing the mixture of each other, and thus forming one—continue their separate and undivided distinctness for miles, till they meet with such rough treatment, from either torrents, wind, or waves, that they join issue, and form at last, one immense river in the St. Lawrence, in which the beautiful but majestic Ottawa is swallowed up.

In the last report on the Geological Survey of Canada, the following remarks on the component parts, and other peculiarities, of the Ottawa and St. Lawrence occur :—

" The water of the Ottawa, containing but little more than one-third as much solid matter as the St. Lawrence, is impregnated with a much larger portion of organic matter, derived from the decomposition of vegetable remains, and a large amount of alkalies uncombined with chlorine or sulphuric acid. Of the alkalies determined as chlorids, the chlorid of potassium in the Ottawa water forms thirty-two per cent., and in that of the St. Lawrence, only sixteen per cent.; while in the former, the silicia equals thirty-four per cent., and in the latter, twenty-three per cent., of the mineral matters. The Ottawa drains a region of crystalline rocks, and receiv s from these by far the greater part of its waters; hence the salts of potash, liberated by the decomposition of these rocks, are in large proportion. The extensive vegetable decomposition, evidenced by the organic matters dissolved in the water, will also have contributed a portion of potash. It will be recollected that the proportion of potash salts in the chlorids of sea-water and saline waters, generally, does not equal more than two or three per cent. As to the St. Lawrence, although the basin of Lake Superior, in which the river takes its origin, is surrounded by ancient sandstones, and by crystalline rocks, it afterwards flows through lakes whose basins are composed of palæozoic strata, which abound in limestones rich in gypsum and salt, and these rocks have given the waters of this river that predominance of soda, chlorine, and sulphuric acid which distinguishes it from the Ottawa. It is an interesting geographical feature of these two rivers, that they each pass through a series of great lakes, in which the waters are enabled to deposit their suspended impurities, and thus are rendered remarkably clear and transparent."

The two rivers thus not mixing at once, is owing, we presume, to the specific gravity of the one being much heavier than that of the other. The two are distinctly seen flowing down together, by the difference in their color.

The lake you are now upon—if a fine morning, and in summer—will be as calm as a mill-pond, and, with its wooded islands, and nicely-wooded country round about, forms a scene of the finest character. Each turn the steamer takes, it opens up with it new beauties. Sometimes, however, the lake, now so placid and beautiful to look upon, is raised like a raging sea, rendering its navigation not so easy, as many a poor raftsman has found to his cost, whilst navigating his treasure of lumber to Quebec or Lachine. You may, possibly, see some of these rafts of lumber as you pass along. Nowhere in the whole of America, we believe, will you see such magnificent and valuable rafts of lumber as on the Ottawa. The rafts on the Delaware, Ohio, and Mississippi, which we have seen, are nothing to com-parts to them—either in size or in the value of the wood of which they are composed. (See *Lumber and Lumbermen.*)

Passing onwards on the lake, you will observe THE INDIAN VILLAGE, at the base of the Two Mountains. There reside the remnants of two tribes, the Iroquois and Algonquins. On the sandy soil behind the village, the Indians have their games, foot races, etc., etc. After passing there, the steamer will probably stop at VAUDREUL, at the head of the Lake of the Two Mountains. Proceeding on from there, the steamer will steer for Point Anglais, (English Point,) and from there cross over to the settlement of REGAUD, and a hill of the same name, on the river Le Graisse.

After enjoying the beauties of the scene on every side, you will shortly find yourself at Carrillon. Opposite Carrillon is situated Point Fortune, the station which leads per stage to the Caledonia Springs, unless passengers wish to go there from L'Original, which you will reach, by-and-by, by taking the cars at Carrillon, the point you have now reached.

At Carrillon you will leave the steamer, walk up to the train which is in readiness to convey you from there to Grenville. On alighting from the steamer, look after your baggage—see it placed on the cart which is to convey it from there to the train—and then see it placed on the train.

You will have a few minutes to wait at Carrillon, during which time you can be surveying the beauties of the scene around you—and get a peep of the rapids which here pass from Grenville to Carrillon, where you are.

"All aboard," as the conductor says; the bell on the engine rings, and you are on the high road to Grenville.

This road passes through farms in all stages of clearing—the numerous shanties betokening that they are held by their original proprietors, who are struggling to see them all cleared some day, and present a very different scene from what they do at present. Passing through, therefore—dismal enough swamp—some good land—farms cleared and uncleared—you arrive at Chatham Station (C. E). You will remember that you are now in Canada East—the other side of the River Ottawa, all the way up, nearly to its source, being Canada West; you, no doubt, are aware that Canada East is inhabited chiefly by French Canadians, (Roman Catholics,) and Canada West chiefly by British, or descendants of such, (and mostly Protestants,) the Scotch people forming a large portion of the population in Canada West. Passing Chatham Station—and a good many cleared farms in its neighborhood—you shortly reach Grenville, where the train stops, and you take the steamer "Phœnix." Here again look after your baggage, and see it on board.

At Grenville, you cannot fail to be forcibly struck with the beauty of the scenery now disclosed to your view. Not being of a poetical disposition, we regret our inability to do it that justice, in our description of it, to which it is entitled. From this point, the steamer turns round, to start on towards Ottawa, 58 miles off (6½ hours). To our mind, this is the finest scene on the whole trip. The Ottawa here forms a sort of bay, with exquisitely beautiful scenery all round it—on one side a range of hills, stretching along as far as the eye can carry, wooded to their tops. The scenery reminds us of the vicinity of Ellen's Isle, on Loch Katrine, (Scot.,) only, that on the Ottawa, at this point, the hills are wooded—whilst those of the Scottish lake are barren—or covered only with pasture and heather.

Passing on from this charming point of view, the steamer now goes direct up the river for Ottawa City, making several stops by the way: the first is Hartwick's old landing, next, L'Original, with its excellent pier, and pretty, quiet little town in the distance.

Proceeding on, you will pass, on the right hand or north side of the river, the lands of the Papineau Seigniory, belonging to L. J. Papineau, of 1837 Canadian rebellion notoriety. This gentleman, we believe, still strongly adheres to his republican opinions, and is not a member in the Canadian legislature, at present. Before the rebellion alluded to, Mr. Papineau held the office of Speaker, and at the time of the rebellion, it is said government was due him about $4,000, which, on the restoration of peace, etc., he received on his return from exile, notwithstanding that he had been one of the leaders in that movement, in 1837.

The seigniory extends for about 15 miles, and is considered one of the poorest in Canada. As you pass on, you will observe the beautiful range of hills, to the north, which, from the different sizes and shapes they assume, present, with their shrubbery, a beautiful fringe work, to the scene all around. These hills form part of the chain, which range from Labrador, all the way to the Rocky Mountains.

Passing the stopping point of Montebello, you will observe Mr. Papineau's residence, embosomed amongst trees and shrubbery of beautiful foliage. It is called Papineau's Castle —Cape St. Marie. At this point, the steamer turns to the left, leaving the hills referred to, behind you. From Mr. Papineau's house, a most magnificent view of the river, and surrounding country, must be had—occupying so prominent a position, at the head of the river, which there forms a sort of bay.

Proceeding on, you will now observe that the scenery assumes rather a different aspect, but still beautiful in its character. You sail past little islands wooded all over, and on between the banks of the river—which in some places become very flat, with the river extending in amongst the forest. At a more advanced season of the year, the river is lower, consequently, much of the water previously spread over a great portion of the country, recedes during the summer months, and before the winter season sets in, a heavy crop of hay is reaped. For nearly eight months in the year, however, the ground is thus covered with the swelling of the river, and of course only fit for cultivation during the hot season of about four months' duration.

You are now approaching to a place about twenty-eight miles of Ottawa—called Thurso —which presents nothing particular but an immense yard full of sawn lumber, belonging to the greatest lumbering establishment in the world—Pollok, Gilmour & Co., of Glasgow, (Scotland,) being one of the many stations which that firm have in Canada, for carrying on their immense trade. From off immense tracts of land, which they hold from government for a mere trifle—situated in different districts on the Ottawa—they have the lumber brought to wharves on the river, made into rafts and then floated down; that intended for the ports on the St. Lawrence and United States, to the west of Montreal, going via Lachine, whilst the greater proportion goes via the route you have been travelling—over the rapids and down to Lake St. Peter's, on the St. Lawrence, till it finally reaches Quebec. There it is sold or shipped by them to ports in Great Britain, large quantities of it finding its way to the Clyde (Scotland). Opposite to Thurso, will be observed what is called Foxe's Point. An English family of that name have settled there, and to this day they appear not to have forgot their taste for neat, well-trimmed grounds, fences, etc., exhibiting many of the characteristics of an Englishman's home. Passing on, you next stop at probably the wharf for Buckingham, (C. E.,) 17 miles inland. Opposite to this landing is Cumberland, (C. W.); passing which, you will shortly reach Gill's wharf, 6 miles from Ottawa, and the last stopping-place previous to reaching there.

In half an hour or so, you will observe the bluffs of Ottawa in the distance, but no appearance of the city, it being situated on ground high above the level of the river, where you land at. To the left you will notice the beautiful little waterfall of the Rideau—a Niagara in miniature—with its Goat Island between the horse shoe and straight line fall. It falls about 30 feet, and forms one of the prettiest little falls to be seen almost anywhere. On the right hand, you will observe a cluster of wooden shanties, at the mouth of the river Gatineau, which there joins the Ottawa, and, as you stand admiring the beauty of the scenery before, behind, and around you, the steamer touches at the wharf of Ottawa City. From the deck of the steamer, you will have an excellent view of the suspension bridge and the Chauderie Falls in the distance, with the rapids and the falls, throwing up the spray all around, forming a white cloud over the bridge. At the wharf you will find vehicles waiting to convey you to any hotel or address you may wish to go to. On reaching the top of the steep incline from the steamer, you will then obtain a first sight, perhaps, of Ottawa City, which was to have been the seat of the Canadian Government—and which may be yet—should the whim or interest of the members of the provincial parliament not decree otherwise.

TRIP UP THE OTTAWA.

The steamer "Lady Simpson," from Lachine to Grenville, is partly owned by its captain—Sheppard.

The steamer " Phœnix"—on board which you will find an excellent dinner for fifty cents, (2s. stg.,)—is commanded by a very civil and obliging Scotchman named McLachlan—who will be glad to point out to you the beauties of the river. From Grenville to Ottawa—a French-Canadian pilot takes charge of the steering of the vessel.

Parties who go to Ottawa City—by rail, via Prescott—as described elsewhere, can return *from* Ottawa by the route now described, and we have no doubt they will be pleased with one of the finest river trips we have experienced in America. The scenery of the Ottawa, just described, is by no means so bold in character as that of the noble river Hudson, from New York to Albany and Troy—still, it is one which cannot fail to afford the highest satisfaction to the tourist.

For bolder scenery, and the highlands of the Ottawa—see next page for account of the Upper Ottawa—being a continuation of the same river from Ottawa—away north-west —extending to parts as yet untrod by few, if any, white men—far less by tourists.

MONTREAL TO OTTAWA, C. W.

VIA GRAND TRUNK RAILROAD.

TAKE the cars on the Grand Trunk Railroad from station in Griffin Town, 1¼ miles from post-office, Montreal. Started from the station, you proceed, getting a fine view of the St. Lawrence on the left, the mountain on the right, and the fine landscape stretching beyond, till you reach Point Claire—16 miles. Leaving there, you proceed on through a beautiful country till you reach the magnificent bridge which crosses the river Ottawa at St. Anne's, going over which you get a hasty glance of the Ottawa stretching far beyond to the west, assuming the appearance of a magnificent lake, situated in a basin, surrounded by finely-wooded hills in the background, andr ichly-wooded country on every side of it. Immediately under this bridge you may observe the rapids rushing along, and also the locks where the steamer for the Ottawa River, from Lachine, passes through to avoid these —called "St. Anne's rapids"—from the name of the village close by.

You pass on to Vaudreuil, 24 miles; Cedars, 29 miles; Coteau Landing, 37 miles; River Beaudette, 44 miles; Lancaster, 64 miles; Summerstown, 60 miles; Cornwall, 68 miles; Moulinette, 73 miles; Dickinson Landing, 77 miles; Aultsville, 84 miles; Williamsburg, 92 miles; Matilda, 99 miles; Edwardsburg, 104 miles, to Prescott Junction, 112 miles from Montreal.

At Prescott Junction, you change cars, and take those on the line from Prescott to Ottawa, 54 miles distant, stopping at eight stations between these points. The stranger, if newly arrived, either via Quebec, or New York, from Great Britain, or continent of Europe, will, on this line, get the first glimpse, most likely, of " bush life," of " shanties," and " cleared," or " partially cleared" lands. The line being a succession of dense forest, swamp, and partially cleared farms, presents few or no interesting features to the tourist farther than those mentioned. Between the last station (Gloucester) and Ottawa (11 miles off) the country presents a much more cleared appearance, and a few well-cultivated farms will be seen along the line of railroad, until it arrives at the station, close to New Edinburgh, on the one side of the Rideau River, with Ottawa on the other side, about a quarter of a mile off.

You will find vehicles in waiting, which will convey yourself and luggage to whatever hotel you please. Campbell's Hotel, Ottawa, we can recommend.

For description of Ottawa, see elsewhere.

After you have visited Ottawa, its river above the town, etc., etc., you can return to Montreal, via steamer on the River Ottawa, via Grenville, Lachine, etc., (see Montreal to Ottawa, via Lachine and steamer,) or the way you came.

45

UNITED STATES TO OTTAWA, C. W.

PRESCOTT JUNCTION, on the Grand Trunk Railway, 112 miles from Montreal, is the nearest point for tourists and emigrants from the United States.

Prescott is approached by steamer from Ogdensburg, opposite side of the river.

Or via rail to Cape Vincent, thence steamer to Kingston, and rail to Prescott.

Or via steamer all the way, viz., Cape Vincent, passing through the Thousand Islands, past Brockville on to Prescott.

Or via steamer to Brockville, thence rail to Prescott Junction. ●

From Prescott to Ottawa proceed per rail, as mentioned in preceding route. See "Montreal to Ottawa," per Grand Trunk Railroad.

From Suspension Bridge or Niagara Falls, per Great Western Rail to Toronto, and thence Grand Trunk Railroad to Prescott Junction; thence, rail. Or steamer from Lewiston or Niagara to Toronto, and thence, steamer on Canada side, or by the American line of steamers from Lewiston and Niagara direct to Brockville or Ogdensburg.

⤳ THE UPPER RIVER OTTAWA. ⤳

A DESCRIPTION of the lower portion of the Ottawa we have given elsewhere, in a trip from Montreal to Ottawa, leaving the river on reaching the town of Ottawa.

For an authentic description of the upper portion of this wonderful river, we annex particulars regarding it, from a report made to the House of Assembly, some time ago. The description of the river which follows, commences *at the source* of the river, and proceeds on *towards Ottawa*, till it reaches the point we left off at:

The length of the course of the Ottawa River is about 780 miles. From its source it bends in a south-west course, and after receiving several tributaries from the height of land separating its waters from the Hudson's Bay, it enters Lake Temiscaming. From its entrance into this lake downward the course of the Ottawa has been surveyed, and is well known.

At the head of the lake the Blanch River falls in, coming about 90 miles from the north. Thirty-four miles farther down the lake it receives the Montreal River, coming 120 miles from the north-west. Six miles lower down on the east, or Lower Canada bank, it receives the Keepawasippi, a large river, which has its origin in a lake of great size, hitherto but partially explored, and known as Lake Keepawa. This lake is connected with another chain of irregularly-shaped lakes, from one of which proceeds the River du Moine, which enters the Ottawa about 100 miles below the mouth of the Keepawasippi, the double discharge from the same chain of lakes in opposite directions, presents a phenomenon similar to the connection between the Orinoco and Rio Negro in South America.

From the Long Sault at the foot of Lake Temiscaming, 233 miles above Bytown, and 360 miles from the mouth of the Ottawa, down to Deux Joachim Rapids, at the head of the Deep River, that is for 89 miles, the Ottawa, with the exception of 17 miles below the Long Sault. and some other intervals, is not at present navigable, except for canoes. Besides other tributaries in the interval, at 197 miles from Ottawa, it receives on the west side the Mattawan, which is the highway for canoes going to Lake Huron, by Lake Nipissing. From the Mattawan the Ottawa flows east by south to the head of Deep River Reach, 9 miles above which it receives the River Du Moine from the north.

From the head of Deep River—as this part of the Ottawa is called—to the foot of Upper Allumette Lake, 2 miles below the village of Pembroke, is an uninterrupted reach of navigable water, 43 miles in length. The general direction of the river, in this part, is south-east. The mountains along the north side of Deep River are upwards of 1000 *feet in height*, and the many wooded islands of Allumette Lake render the scenery of this part of the Ottawa magnificent and picturesque—even said to surpass the celebrated Lake of the Thousand Islands on the St. Lawrence.

south-east through Coulonge Lake, and passing behind the nearly similar Islands of Calumet, to the head of the Calumet Falls, the Ottawa presents, with the exception of one slight rapid, a reach of 50 miles of navigable water. The mountains on the north side of Coulonge Lake, which rise apparently to the height of 1500 feet, add a degree of grandeur to the scenery, which is, in other respects, beautiful and varied. In the Upper Allumettes Lake, 1500 miles from Ottawa, the river receives from the west the Petawawee, one of its largest tributaries. This river is 140 miles in length, and drains an area of 2,200 square miles. At Pembroke, 9 miles lower down on the same side, an inferior stream, the Indian River, also empties itself into the Ottawa.

At the head of Lake Coulonge, the Ottawa receives from the north the Black River, 180 miles in length, draining an area of 1120 miles; and 9 miles lower, on the same side, the River Coulonge, which is probably 160 miles in length, with a valley of 1800 square miles.

From the head of the Calumet Falls, to Portage du Fort, the head of the steamboat navigation, a distance of 80 miles, are impassible rapids. Fifty miles above the city the Ottawa receives on the west the Bonechere, 110 miles in length, draining an area of 980 miles. Eleven miles lower, it receives the Madawaska, one of its greatest feeders, a river 210 miles in length, and draining 4,100 square miles.

Thirty-seven miles above Ottawa, there is an interruption in the navigation, caused by 3 miles of rapids and falls, to pass which a railroad has been made. At the foot of the rapids, the Ottawa divides among islands.

Six miles above Ottawa begins the rapids, terminating in the Chaudière Falls, Ottawa. The greatest height of the Chaudière Falls is about 40 feet.

TRIP TO THE RIVER SAGUENAY.

For about $12, a trip can be enjoyed to and from one of the most magnificent districts in Canada—where nature appears in all her wild and secluded grandeur.

Tourists take the steamer from Quebec, which sails generally every Wednesday.

To quote from one who visited this district, "You leave in the morning, and passing down the St. Lawrence, put in at several places for passengers, which gives an opportunity of seeing the *habitans*, and the old-fashioned French settlements of St. Thomas, River Ouelle, Kamouraska, and many others, together with Orleans Island, Crane Island, Goose Island, and the Pilgrims. The north and south shores of the river are thickly studded with parish churches, having spires of tin which glitter in the sun like shining silver ; these, and the whitewashed farm-houses, form two objects characteristic of Lower Canada. By sunset you arrive at River du Loup. The water is quite salt, and the river, expanding to the breadth of 20 miles, gives it the appearance of an open sea ; and it is much frequented as a sea-bathing place.

" Here you remain all night on board, so as to be ready for an early start at dawn, when you stretch across for the north shore, steering for a great gap in the mountains. This is the mouth of the Saguenay, one of the most singular rivers in the world; not a common river, with undulating banks and shelving shores, and populous villages: not a river precipitous on one side, and rolling land on the other, formed by the washing away of the mountains for ages: this is not a river of that description. It is perfectly straight, with a sheer precipice on each side, without any windings, or projecting bluffs, or sloping banks, or sandy shores. It is as if the mountain range had been cleft asunder, leaving a horrid gulf of 60 miles in length, and 4000 feet in depth, through the grey mica-schist, and still looking new and fresh. 1500 feet of this is perpendicular cliff, often too steep and solid for the hemlock or dwarf oak to find root ; in which case, being covered with coloured lichens and moss, these fresh-looking fractures often look, in shape and colour, like painted fans, and are called the Pictured Rocks. But those parts, more slanting, are thickly covered with stunted trees, spruce and maple, and birch, growing wherever they can find crevices to extract nourishment: and the bare roots of the oak, grasping the rock, have a resemblance to gigantic claws. The base of these cliffs lie far under water, to an unknown depth. For many miles from its mouth, no soundings have been obtained with 2000 feet of line, and for the entire distance of 60 miles, until you reach Ha-ha Bay, the largest ships can sail without obstruction from banks or shoals, and on reaching the extremity of the bay, can drop their anchor in 30 fathoms.

"The view up this river is singular in many respects; hour after hour, as you sail along, precipice after precipice unfolds itself to view, as in a moving panorama, and you sometimes forget the size and height of the objects you are contemplating, until reminded by seeing a ship of 1000 tons lying like a small pinnace under the towering cliff to which she is moored; for, even in these remote and desolate regions, industry is at work, and, although you cannot much discern it, saw-mills have been built on some of the tributary streams which fall into the Saguenay. But what strikes one most, is the absence of beach or strand; for except in a few places where mountain torrents, rushing through gloomy ravines, have washed down the detritus of the hills, and formed some alluvial land at the mouth, no coves, nor creeks, nor projecting rocks are seen in which a boat could find shelter, or any footing be obtained. The characteristic is a steep wall of rock, rising abruptly from the water—a dark and desolate region, where all is cold and gloomy; the mountains hidden with driving mist, the water black as ink, and cold as ice. No ducks nor sea-gulls sitting on the water, or screaming for their prey; no hawks nor eagles soaring overhead, although there is abundance of what might be called 'Eagle Cliffs;' no deer coming down to drink at the streams; no squirrels nor birds to be seen among the trees; no fly on the water, nor swallow skimming over the surface. It reminds you of

'That lake whose gloomy shore
Sky-lark never warbled o'er.'

One living thing you may see, but it is a cold-blooded animal; you may see the cold seal, spreading himself upon his clammy rock, watching for his prey. And this is all you see for the first 20 miles, save the ancient settlement of Tadousac at the entrance, and the pretty cove of L'Ance a l'Eau, which is a fishing station.

"Now you reach Cape Eternité, Cape Trinité, and many other overhanging cliffs, remarkable for having such clean fractures, seldom equalled for boldness and effect, which create constant apprehensions of danger, even in a calm; but if you happen to be caught in a thunder-storm, the roar, and darkness, and flashes of lightning are perfectly appalling. At last you terminate your voyage at Ha-ha Bay, that is, smiling or laughing bay in the Indian language, for you are perfectly charmed and relieved to arrive at a beautiful spot where you have sloping banks, a pebbly shore, boats and wherries, and vessels riding at anchor, birds and animals, a village, a church, French Canadians and Scottish Highlanders, and in short, there is nothing can remind one more of a scene in Argyleshire.

"The day is now half spent; you have been ashore, looking through the village, examining into the nature of what appears a very thriving settlement; the inhabitants seem to be all French and Scotch, understanding each other's language, and living in perfect amity. You hear that Mr. Price, of Quebec, is the gentlemen to whom all this improvement is due. That it is he who has opened up the Saguenay country, having erected many saw-mills, each the nucleus of a village, and that a trade in sawed lumber is carried on to the extent of 100 ship loads in the season. The river is navigable for ships as far as Chicoutimi, about 70 miles from its mouth. An extensive lumbering establishment is there, and the timber is collected in winter through all the neighbouring country, as far as Lake St. John, which is 50 miles further up, and is the grand source of the Saguenay.

"After having seen and heard all this, you get on board, weigh anchor, pass again down the river, reviewing the solemn scene, probably meeting neither vessel, boat nor canoe, through all the dreary way, and arrive at the mouth of the river in time to cross to River

THE FALLS OF MONTMORENCI.

du Loup, where you again find a safe harbour for the night. Next day you again pass up the St. Lawrence, stopping for a short time at Murray Bay, a beautiful grassy valley on the north shore, surrounded by wooded mountains, and much frequented by Quebec families, as a bathing place. You arrive at Quebec in the evening, thus taking just 3 days for your excursion, at an expense of about $12."

FALLS OF MONTMORENCI, NEAR QUEBEC.

Few strangers visit Quebec without going to see the Falls of Montmorenci. These Falls, which are situated in a beautiful nook of the river, are higher than those of Niagara, being more than two hundred and fifty feet; but they are very narrow, being only some fifty feet wide. This place is a very celebrated focus of winter amusements. During the frost, the spray from the Falls accumulates to such an extent as to form a cone of some eighty feet high. There is also a second cone of inferior altitude, and it is this of which visitors make the most use, as being less dangerous than the higher one. They carry "toboggins,"—long, thin pieces of wood—and having arrived at the summit, place themselves on these and slide down with immense velocity. Ladies and gentlemen both enter with equal spirit into this amusement. It requires much skill to avoid accidents; but sometimes people do tumble heels over head to the bottom. They generally drive to this spot in sleighs, taking their wine and provisions with them; and upon the pure white cloth which nature has spread out for them, they partake of their dainty repast and enjoy a most agreeable pic-nic. One does not feel in the least cold, as the exercise so thoroughly warms and invigorates the system. The distance of these Falls from Quebec is eight miles.

49

CITY OF QUEBEC—CANADA EAST.

ASSOCIATED as Quebec is with so many scenes of military glory, of success as well as defeat, it must at all times possess a peculiar interest to almost every one. On its fields, and

around its battlements, some of the bravest of the sons of Great Britain and Ireland, America and France, have fallen, and around its citadel, some of the most daring exploits have taken place. Standing on a bold and precipitous promontory, Quebec has not inappropriately been called the "Gibraltar of America," with which the names of the brave Wolfe, Montcalm, and Montgomery must ever remain connected.

The citadel stands on what is called Cape Diamond, 350 feet above the level of the sea, and includes about 40 acres of ground. The view from off the citadel is of the most picturesque and grand character. There will be seen the majestic St. Lawrence, winding its course for about 40 miles, whilst the background of the panoramic scene is filled up by extensive plains, running backwards to lofty mountains in the distance, with Point Levi opposite, and the Island of Orleans in the distance, whilst the junction of the River St. Charles, and the Great River, form that magnificent sheet of water, where numerous vessels are to be seen riding at anchor during the summer season.

A walk around the ramparts of the citadel will well repay the stranger, by a magnificent change of scene at every turn he takes. The city itself bears all the resemblance of a strongly fortified and ancient city, and, in that respect, so very different from the newly sprung-up cities, westward. The streets are generally narrow, and, in some parts, very steep, in walking from Lower Town to Upper Town, more particularly. Lower Town is where all the shipping business of the port is carried on, chiefly lumber—in export—and every description of goods—in import. At Quebec, the greater portion of the immense lumber-district of the Ottawa finds a market; vessels coming to Quebec, in ballast and cargo, return with the logs, staves, and deals of the up-country. The population of Quebec is largely infused with French Canadians, and in passing along its streets, nothing, almost, but the French language is heard.

The most interesting places and objects of interest in and around Quebec will be found as follows:—

The Plains of Abraham, a short way out of the city, westward, where the celebrated battle was fought between the troops of Britain and France, led by their heroes Wolfe and Montcalm. A monument is erected on the spot where Wolfe fell, with the inscription, " Here Wolfe died victorious."

The Citadel, situated on the highest point of Cape Diamond, and commanding the most extensive view to be had.

The Esplanade, between the ramparts and D'Autueil street, used for drilling the troops.

DURHAM TERRACE AND THE CITADEL, QUEBEC.

The Public, or Palace Garden, in Upper Town, fronts Des Carriers street. One of the most interesting objects of historical interest is the granite monument erected to the joint memory of the two opposing heroes, Wolfe and Montcalm, who both fell in battle. It is placed in what is called the Palace Garden, finely shaded with trees. It was erected in 1827; the Earl of Dalhousie, then Governor-general of Canada, laying the foundation-stone amid great masonic honors. The chaste design of the monument, which is 65 feet high, is

WOLFE AND MONTCALM'S MONUMENT.

QUEBEC.

from the pencil of Captain Young, 79th Highlanders, and the concise but eloquent inscription is by Dr. J. C. Fisher, at one time connected with the Quebec press, for which inscription he was awarded a gold medal. It reads as follows:

WOLFE—MONTCALM.

MORTEM VIRTUS COMMUNEM;

FAMAM HISTORIA;

MONUMENTUM POSTERITAS.

DEDIT.

A. D. 1827.

Which, being rendered into English, means: "Military virtue gave them a common death history a common fame; posterity a common monument."

QUEBEC.

Durham Terrace, from which one of the finest and most extensive views is to be had. A great resort of the citizens during the cool evenings of summer. At one time the site of the Castle of St. Louis.

The Marine Hospital, situated on the peninsula near Cartier's Bay; the spot where Jacques Cartier the discoverer of the St. Lawrence, spent the winter of 1535 and '36.

The Ruins of the Intendant Palace, near Craig street, may interest the antiquary in such matters. *Montcalm's Head-quarters*, on the heights of Beauport, a short way east of Beauport's Mills. *Montmorenci House*, situated close to the bank of the river, near the Falls of Montmorenci, once the residence of the late Duke of Kent, father of her present Majesty Queen Victoria. *The Quebec Exchange*, an excellent reading-room, well supplied with Canadian, American and British newspapers. Free to strangers.

The University of Quebec, Hope street, Upper Town, a massive gray stone building.

Court House and City Hall, St. Louis street.

Jail, corner of Ann street. Cost £60,000 ($300,000).

The Jesuit Barracks, Lunatic Asylum, Music Hall, and the Protestant and Catholic churches form the remainder of the principal buildings in the city.

"A morning's ramble to the Plains of Abraham will not fail to recall historical recollections and to gratify a taste for beautiful scenery. On leaving the St. Louis Gate, let the traveller ascend the counterscarp on the left, that leads to the *glacis* of the citadel; and hence pursuing a direction to the right, let him approach one of the Martello Towers, whence he may enjoy a beautiful view of the St. Lawrence. A little beyond let him ascend the right bank, and he reaches the celebrated Plains of Abraham, near the spot where General Wolfe fell. On the highest ground, surrounded by wooden fences, can clearly be traced out the redoubt where he received the fatal wound. He was carried a few yards in the rear, and placed against a rock till he expired. It has since been removed. Within an enclosure lower down, and near to the road, is the stone well from which they brought him water. The English right nearly faced this redoubt, and on this position the French left rested. The French army arrived on the Plains from the right of this position, as it came from Beauport, and not from Quebec; and, on being defeated, retired down the heights by which it had ascended, and not into Quebec. In front of the Plains from this position stands the house of Marchmont. It is erected on the sight of a French redoubt that once defended the ascent from Wolfe's Cove. Here landed the British army under Wolfe's command, and, on mounting the banks, carried this detached work. The troops in the garrison are usually reviewed on the Plains. The tourist may farther enjoy a beautiful ride. Let him leave by St. Louis Gate and pass the Plains, and he will arrive at Marchmont, the property of John Gilmour, Esq. The former proprietor, Sir John Harvey, went to considerable expense in laying out the grounds in a pleasing and tasteful manner. His successor, Sir Thomas Noel Hill, also resided here, and duly appreciated its beauties. The view in front of the house is grand. Here the river widens, and assumes the appearance of a lake, whose surface is enlivened by numerous merchant-ships at anchor, and immense rafts of timber floating down. On leaving Marchmont he will pass some beautiful villas, whose park-like grounds remind one of England, and from some points in which are commanded views worthy of a painter's study. Among these villas may be mentioned Wolfesfield, Spencer Wood, and Woodfield. The last was originally built by the Catholic Bishop of Samos, and, from the several additions made by subsequent proprietors, had a somewhat irregular, though picturesque appearance. It was burnt down, and rebuilt in a fine regular style. It is now the residence of James Gibb, Esq.

"In this neighbourhood is situated Mount Hermon Cemetery. It is about three miles from Quebec, on the south side of the St. Lewis road, and slopes irregularly but beautifully down the cliff which overhangs the St. Lawrence. It is thirty-two acres in extent, and the grounds were tastefully laid out by the late Major Douglass, U. S. Engineers, whose taste and skill had been previously shown in the arrangement of Greenwood Cemetery, near New York."

Leaving this beautiful locality, the walk continues to the woods, on the edge of the banks rising from the shore.

The tourist, instead of returning by a road conducting through a wood into St. Louis Road for Quebec, would do better by continuing his ride to the Church of St. Foy, from which is seen below the St. Charles, gliding smoothly through a lovely valley, whose sides rise gradually to the mountains, and are literally covered with habitations. The villages of Lorette and Charlesbourg are conspicuous objects. Before entering the suburb of St. John, on the banks of the St. Charles stands the General Hospital, designed, as the name implies, for the disabled and sick of every description.

A day's excursion to Indian Lorette and Lake St. Charles would gratify, we doubt not, many a tourist. It will be necessary to leave by 6 o'clock, A. M., and to take provisions for the trip. After leaving the Palace Gate, the site of the former intendant's palace is passed. Mr. Bigot was the last intendant who resided in it.

The most pleasant road to Lorette is along the banks of the St. Charles. On arriving at the village, the best view is on the opposite bank. The fall is in the foreground, and the church and village behind. The villagers claim to be descended from those Hurons, to whom the French monarch, in 1651, gave the seigniory of Sillery. In the wars between the French and English, the Hurons contributed much to the success of the former, as they were one of the most warlike tribes among the aborigines of this continent. At present, they are a harmless, quiet set of people, drawing only part of their subsistence from fishing and hunting. A missionary is maintained by government for their religious instruction, and the schoolmaster belongs to the tribe. Here may be purchased bows and arrows, and moccasins very neatly ornamented by the squaws.

On arriving at Lake St. Charles, by embarking in a double canoe, the tourist will have his taste for picturesque mountain scenery gratified in a high degree. The lake is four miles long, and one broad, and is divided into two parts by projecting ledges. The lake abounds in trout, so that the angling tourist may find this spot doubly inviting. On the route back to the city, the village of Charlesbourg is passed. It is one of the oldest and most interesting settlements in Canada. It has two churches, one of which is the centre of the surrounding farms, whence they all radiate. The reason for this singular disposal of the allotments, arose from the absolute necessity of creating a neighbourhood. For this purpose, each farm was permitted to occupy only a space of three acres in front by thirty in depth. The population was in these days scanty, and labourers were difficult to be procured. By this arrangement, a road was more equally kept up in front of each farm, and it was the duty of every proprietor to preserve such road. Another advantage was the proximity of the church, whence the bell sounded the tocsin of alarm, whenever hostile attempts were made by the Indians, and where the inhabitants rallied in defence of their possessions.

Within the citadel are the various magazines, store-houses, and other buildings required for the accommodation of a numerous garrison; and immediately overhanging the precipice to the south, in a most picturesque situation, looking perpendicularly downwards, on the river, stands a beautiful row of buildings, containing the mess rooms and barracks for the officers, their stables, and spacious kitchens. The fortifications, which are continued round the whole of the Upper Town, consist of bastions connected by lofty curtains of solid masonry, and ramparts from 25 to 35 feet in height, and about the same in thickness, bristling with heavy cannon, round towers, loophole walls, and massive gates recurring at certain distances. On the summit of the ramparts, from Cape Diamond to the Artillery Barracks, is a broad covered way, or walk, used as a place of recreation by the inhabitants, and commanding a most agreeable view of the country towards the west. This passes over the top of St. John's and St. Louis Gate, where there is stationed a sergeant's guard. Above St. John's Gate, there is at sunset one of the most beautiful views imaginable. The St. Charles gambolling, as it were, in the rays of the departing luminary, the light still lingering on the spires of Lorette and Charlesbourg, until it fades away beyond the lofty mountains of *Bonhomme* and *Tsounonthuan*, present an evening scene of gorgeous and surpassing splendour. The city, being defended on its land side by its ramparts, is protected on the other sides by a lofty wall and parapet, based on the cliff, and commencing near the St. Charles at the Artillery Barracks. These form a very extensive range of buildings, the part within the Artillery Gate being occupied as barracks by the officers and men of that distinguished corps, with a guard and mess room. The part without the gate is used as magazines, store-houses, and offices for the ordnance department.

The circuit of the fortifications, enclosing the Upper Town, is two miles and three-quarters; the total circumference outside the ditches and space reserved by government, on which no house can be built on the west side, is about 3 miles.

Founded upon a rock, and in its highest parts overlooking a great extent of country—between 300 and 400 miles from the ocean—in the midst of a great continent, and yet displaying fleets of foreign merchantmen in its fine capacious bay, and showing all the bustle of a crowded sea-port—its streets narrow, populous, and winding up and down almost mountainous declivities—situated in the latitude of the finest parts of Europe—exhibiting in its environs the beauty of an European capital—and yet, in winter, smarting with the cold of Siberia—governed by a people of different language and habits from the mass of the population—opposed in religion, and yet leaving that population without taxes, and in the full enjoyment of every privilege, civil and religious. Such are the prominent features which strike a stranger in the City of Quebec!"

The stranger can have no difficulty in finding the various places and objects of interest in, and around the city, and by taking a *caleche*, and making a bargain beforehand, will be able to see a great deal in little time, and at no great cost.

For particulars of the Falls of Montmorenci, and River Saguenay, see preceeding pages.

WHITE MOUNTAINS, NEW HAMPSHIRE.

THE accomplished author of "America and the Americans" thus writes regarding this portion of the United States:—"This is one of the wildest regions in the United States. From the top of the stage we have a wide prospect over forests, pastoral valleys, ravines, and dingles; Mount Lafayette rising before us in solemn majesty, and behind us, far as the eye can reach, an undulating country, stretching away towards the frontiers of Canada. For the first 3 miles the drive lies through a tangled wood, and up an ascent so steep that our team occasionally pauses. The road is so narrow that the trees touch the carriage on both sides at the same time, a . so rough that passengers hold on firmly f heir lives; yet the coachman drives his . hand with the utmost ease and skill."

During nine or ten months of the year, the summits of the mountains are covered with snow and ice, giving them a bright and dazzling appearance. On every side are long and winding gullies, deepening in their descent to the plain below.

These mountains are situated in the county of Coos, in the N. part of the State. They extend about 20 miles, from S. W. to N. E., and are the more elevated parts of a range extending many miles in that direction. Their base is about 10 miles broad, and are the highest in New England; and, if we except the Rocky Mountains, and one or two peaks in North Carolina, they are the most lofty of any in the United States.

Although these mountains are 65 miles distant from the ocean, their snow-white summits are distinctly visible, in good weather, more than 50 miles from shore. Their appearance, at that distance, is that of a silvery cloud skirting the horizon.

The names here given are those generally appropriated to the different summits: *Mount Washington* is known by its superior elevation, and by its being the southern of the three highest peaks. *Mount Adams* is known by its sharp, terminating peak, and being the north of Washington. *Jefferson* is situated between these two. *Madison* is the eastern peak of the range. *Monroe* is the first to the south of Washington. *Franklin* is the second south, and is known by its level surface. *Lafayette* is known by its conical shape, and being the third south of Washington. The ascent to the summits of these mountains, though fatiguing, is not dangerous; and the visitant is richly rewarded for his labour and curiosity. In passing from the Notch to the highest summit, the traveller crosses the summits of Mounts Lafayette, Franklin, and Monroe. In accomplishing this, he must pass through a forest, and cross several ravines. These are neither wide nor deep, nor are they discovered at a great distance; for the trees fill them up exactly even with the mountain on each side, and their branches interlock with each other in such a manner that it is very difficult to pass through them, and they are so stiff and thick as almost to support a man's weight. After crossing Mount Franklin, you pass over the eastern pinnacle of Mount Monroe, and soon find yourself on a plain of some extent, at the foot of Mount Washington. Here is a fine resting-place, on the margin of a beautiful sheet of water, of an oval form, covering about three-fourths of an acre. The waters are pleasant to the taste, and deep. Not a living creature is to be seen in the waters at this height on the hills; nor does vegetation grow in or around them, to obscure t e clear rocky or gravelly bottom on which they rest. A small spring discharges itself into this pond, at its south-east angle. Another pond, of about two-thirds its size, lies north-west of this. Directly before you, the pinnacle of Mount Washington rises with majestic grandeur, like an immense pyramid, or some vast kremlin, in this magnificent city of mountains. The pinnacle is elevated about 1500 feet above the plain, and is composed principally of huge rocks of granite and gneiss, piled together, presenting a variety of colours and forms. The ascent is made on horseback.

In ascending, you must pass enormous masses of loose stone: but a ride of half an hour will generally carry you to the summit. The view from this point is wonderfully grand and picturesque. Innumerable mountains, lakes, ponds, rivers, towns, and villages meet the delighted eye, and the dim Atlantic stretches its waters along the eastern horizon. To the north is seen the lofty summits of Adams and Jefferson; and to the east, a little detached from the range, supported on the north by a high ridge, which extends to Mount Jefferson; on the north-east by a large grassy plain, terminating in a vast spur, extending far away in that direction; east, by a promontory, which breaks off abruptly at St. Anthony's Nose; south and south-east by a grassy plain, in summer, of more than 40 acres. At the south-eastern extremity of this plain a ridge commences, which slopes gracefully away towards the vale of the Saco, upon which, at short distances from each other, arise rocks, resembling in some places, towers; in others, representing the various orders of architecture.

THE SILVER CASCADE.

THESE beautiful falls afford one of the finest sights to be seen in the White Mountains, especially during the season of freshets, when the increased volume of water, as it dashes and leaps down the mountain side in its journey of eight hundred feet to the valley beneath, gratifies the eye of the beholder with the sparkling of its silvery spray, while his ear is no less delighted with the soft music of its motion. When seen on a bright day at the distance of a mile or two, the rays of the sun falling upon and mingling with its dancing waters, it appears exactly like a stream of molten silver burning its way through the mountain forest and over the granite ledges with all the force and speed, but without the anger or destructiveness, with which the heated lava flows from the volcano. In a season of drouth the stream is scanty; but, even in its most shallow condition, it presents innumerable beauties to the true admirer of Nature's jewelry.

THE FLUME.

A SHORT distance from the Flume House is the beautiful cascade from whose name the hotel derives its name. Through a deep ravine, the rocky walls of which are fifty feet high and twenty feet apart, flows the waters of the "Flume" for several hundred feet. In wet seasons the tide rushes impetuously along its channel, but in dry times the bed of the stream enables the visitor to walk its length dry-shod.

THE FLUME HOUSE.

ALTHOUGH the architectural claims of the Flume House are not very imposing, yet the plan of its construction is peculiarly adapted to the absolute *needs* of its travel-worn guests. After a weary jaunt up the mountains, one does not require the additional labor of mounting six pair of stairs to his bed-room—which board in a modern fashionable hotel would compel him to—neither, if he would sit down to rest, or wishes to indulge in a "fragrant Havana," would he enjoy these luxuries within the narrow confines of the said chamber, or in the overcrowded bar-room, with that zeal and relish which he finds under the ample piazza of the Flume House. Therefore, the Flume House is just what it should be; commodious and comfortable, if not grand and magnificent.

Principal Objects of Interest.—In addition to the scenes described on the preceding pages, we will enumerate the following as being worthy especial notice.

The Profile Rock.—On the road through the Notch, a short distance south of the Profile House, there is a point from which the gigantic profile of the "human face divine" is seen protruding from the mountain side. This strange visage, which seems as regular in its outlines as though it had been chiselled from the solid granite by the hand of art, is composed of three distinct masses of rock, one forming the forehead, another the nose and upper lip, and a third the chin. Seen from the point indicated above, the profile is almost faultless, and portrays a strong, stern old man, and is hence called the "Old Man of the Mountain;" while a little lower down the road, the old man is transformed into a "toothless old woman in a mob cap."

The Pool.—This is a deep well at one end of the "Flume," and is sunken by the hand of Nature nearly 200 feet into the solid rock. The depth of water is generally about 40 feet, and from the surface of the water to the surface of the ground 150 feet.

Tuckerman's Ravine is a long deep glen, with rough and jagged walls, often quite inaccessible. It is filled hundreds of feet deep by the winter snows, through which, when summer comes, a gentle brook winds its way, gradually opening a channel until it flows through an immense snow cave, which, on being measured one season, was found to be 180 feet long, 80 feet wide, and 40 feet high.

Lake of the Clouds.—This is the name of a beautiful pond, a short distance from the Warlington House. Its waters are remarkably clear, and on a still, fair day its bosom is as reflective as the most polished mirror.

EAGLE CLIFF.

THE summit of this bold promontory affords to the tourist a magnificent view of the varied freaks of nature which are so plentifully bestowed in this romantic region. Just behind it towers Mount Lafayette, or the great Notch, the highest of the Franconia range, which lifts its aspiring head 5,200 feet above the level of the sea; while in front, and many hundred feet below, its shadow falls upon a beautiful valley, along whose winding paths the moving human beings seem to the spectator from the "cliff" to be but so many little mice hurrying to and fro. This point is a favourite resting-place with tourists, who stop here to breathe awhile, and to draw in fresh inspiration by a prolonged view of the jutting cliffs, the lofty peaks, the silver lakes, the leaping cascades, and the green valleys which stretch, like huge panoramic views, along the whole line of vision.

Echo Lake.—This is a small but beautiful pond, entirely enclosed by high mountains. From this little spot a voice lifted to the ordinary pitch, will be echoed repeatedly several times, while the discharge of a gun comes back like a charge of "heaven's artillery."

The Basin.—This is an object of great interest, and is situated 5 miles south of the Notch. The Basin is 45 feet in diameter, and 28 feet from the edge to the bottom of the water. It is nearly circular, and has been made so by the whirling of rocks round and round by strong currents. The water, as it descends from the Basin, forms a number of beautiful cascades.

Profile Lake.—This is a pretty little body of water a quarter of a mile long, and half as wide. It is just under the "Old Man of the Mountain," and is sometimes called the "Old Man's Washbowl."

The Devil's Den.—This is a mysterious-looking cavern, just opposite the silver cascade, and an object of great interest to the lovers of the marvellous.

Pulpit Rock.—This is supposed to have been, in early times, the point from which the Puritan elders occasionally addressed their people, as on no other hypothesis can its title be accounted for, as it does not in any degree resemble a pulpit of any known pattern.

Oaks Gulf and *Great Gulf* are dark and frightful abysses, the latter of which descends, abrupt and rugged, from near the top of Mount Washington to a depth of 2000 feet.

The Crystal Cascade is situated in a highly romantic spot in a secluded valley, about 3 miles from the Glen House. The fall is 80 feet, and breaks in its descent.

THE WILLEY HOUSE, WHITE MOUNTAINS.

The above house stands upon a spot which will ever remain memorable in the history of the White Mountains, as having been the scene of a fearful calamity which overtook a family named Willey, residing there, who were all buried beneath an avalanche, or slide, from the mountain, which occurred during the year 1826, a year remarkable for a great flood in these mountain regions.

Leaving Willey House, the tourist, who is desirous of ascending higher, will find himself in the vicinity of the "Notch," as it is called.

"The *Notch of the White Mountains* is a phrase appropriated to a very narrow defile, extending two miles in length, between two huge cliffs, apparently rent asunder by some vast convulsion of nature, probably that of the deluge.

"The scenery at this place is exceedingly beautiful and grand. About half a mile from the entrance of the chasm is seen a most beautiful cascade, issuing from a mountain on the right, about 800 feet above the subjacent valley, and about two miles distant. The stream passes over a series of rocks, almost perpendicular, with a course so little broken as to preserve the appearance of a uniform current, and yet so far disturbed as to be perfectly white. This beautiful stream, which passes down a stu-

pendous precipice, is called by Dwight the *Silver Cascade*." It is probably one of the most beautiful in the world, and has been thus described:—

"The stream is scanty, but its course from among the deep forest, whence its springs issue into light, is one of singular beauty. Buried beneath the lofty precipice of the gorge, after ascending through *Pulpit Rock*, by the side of the turbulent torrent of the Saco, the ear is suddenly saluted by the soft dashings of the sweetest of cascades; and a glance upward reveals its silver streams issuing from the loftiest crests of the mountain, and leaping from crag to crag. It is a beautiful vision in the midst of the wildest and most dreary scenery."

Mount Washington House, capable of accommodating 100 guests, is situated about 4 miles from the *Notch*.

The Notch House is at the head of the Saco River, and about 9 miles from the top of Mount Washington.

The Willey House, alluded to above, is about 2 miles below the Notch.

The Crawford House, in the valley of the Saco, is about 8 miles below the Notch, these, together with the

Glen House, will be found in every respect desirable, for stopping at. Particulars of *Tip-Top House* will be found on next page.

TIP-TOP HOUSE, WHITE MOUNTAINS.

As already explained, Mount Washington forms the highest of the range of the White Mountains, 6234 feet above the sea.

We present above, a sketch made from a photograph taken of the highest point of Mount Washington, known by travellers as "Tip-Top House," to attain to which is the ambition of all tourists who make the attempt to climb to the apex of the highest of the range in this region of "the mountain and the flood."

Tip-Top House is a rude built Inn erected under most difficult circumstances, and not without great risk of life and property.

In Tip-Top House, tourists can be accommodated all night, so that any who are desirous of witnessing the setting of the sun, and being up in time for sunrise next morning, can accomplish both, by ascending in the afternoon, staying there all night, and returning next morning. Those who try the experiment, if favoured with a clear morning, will be certain to be repaid for their trouble.

Regarding the view from the summit of this dizzy height, we quote :—

"If the day be clear, a view is afforded unequalled perhaps on the eastern side of the North American continent. Around you are confused masses of mountains, bearing the appearance of a sea of molten lava suddenly cooled whilst its ponderous waves were yet in commotion. On the S. E. horizon gleams a rim of silver light—it is the Atlantic Ocean, 65 miles distant, laving the shores of Maine.

Lakes of all sizes, from Lake Winnipiseogee to mere mountain ponds, and mountains beneath you, gleam misty and wide. Far off in the N. E. is Mount Katahdin. In the western horizon are the Green Mountains of Vermont, while the space is filled up with every kind of landscape—mountain and hill, plain and valley, lake and river."

It would be vain in us to attempt a description of the varied wonders which here astonish and delight the beholder. To those who have visited these mountains, our description would be tame and uninteresting ; and he who has never ascended their hoary summits cannot realize the extent and magnificence of the scene. These mountains are decidedly of primitive formation. Nothing of volcanic origin has ever yet been discovered, on the most diligent research. They have for ages, probably, exhibited the same unvarying aspect. No minerals are here found of much rarity or value. The rock which most abounds is schistose, intermixed with greenstone, mica, granite, and gneiss.

There are several routes to this highland district; amongst the principal, and those which will please the tourist best, we name from Portland, Maine, per Eastern Railroad, or from Boston to Plymouth, thence per coach to the Flume House, thence through Franconia Notch—about 150 miles. Another route, and said to be the finest, is via Lake Winnipiseogee, 180 miles. Proceed from Boston per Boston and Maine and Cocheco Railroad.